Dedication

This is dedicated to my lover and king, through it all we still together sharing a bond that's unbreakable because this love right here is forever. My alpha Perdido Skinny Pearl Cook BKA El Pearl Royal 13 Bey a true moor…. Eternal love poppi…… Also, to all my fans and family thank you for your support

Warning…….

This book contains graphic material with offensive language and actions which are all fiction. Not suitable for anyone under the age 18. If anyone is offended by this material, I apologize a head of time but still enjoy the book anyway…….

Still Here

Back where it all started

Face to face with myself just to see where my heart is at

I stood up to life and all her trials

Held onto what's real and watched the world turn foul

Over the years I tried to do what's right

But sometimes wrong was the only solution in sight

And even then, I tried to make amends

But jealousy and envy kept me losing friends

I never asked for the world to be placed on my shoulders

But held it up for family until it was over

I never gave up, never let nothing brake me, never turned

rotten and didn't let hate make me

Like Alex Haley, I took roots in Henning Tennessee

Walked the true path of my ancestors like Noble Drew Ali

Like Ninesun Bey, I feel their pain

And Never forgot my elders, so I honor their name

I never sold out or hated on my brothers

Tried to tell them what's real but they were worshipping

others

See I been through it all

I walked through hell

I was forged in fire just to earn my "El"

That's a lesson in life for ya'll who don't know

Cause through all the evil I continued to grow

I beat the odds and though my life been rocky I went hard

and didn't let nothing stop me

I kept it true to life cause my love been bliss and through

all that I found my genesis

A new beginning, a change in direction from the path I was

living

Did over two decades straight and I'm still here, still whole

Unbreakable nature, Elohim soul

9.13

~El Pearl Royal 13 Bey

Prologue

"You" Nemis whispered while holding on to me like her life depended on it. I understood her fear. She has been stuck in that panic room for days and probably the fear of never being found settled in her.

"It's ok Nem I got you and your safe" I said to her in a calm tone. My heart on the other hand was anything but. I wasn't sure I would make it too her in time before the supplies ran out, but I knew that she was safe in that panic room. My ole dude never did shit half ass when it came to his kids. I stood up with her in my arms because I knew she was afraid to let go. The fear of worrying if I was going to disappear showed on her face. A little girl should never have to worry about such things. It saddens me because she did. To be so young she was thrown into a world wind of chaos without the knowledge or tools to take care of herself. Besides, she shouldn't have to.

"Nemis, I need you to tuck your face in my neck honey. I don't want you to see"

"The smell" she replied with a shaky voice. She was about to cry, and I hated that. She knows what happened. "Breath through your mouth baby girl. We have to get your stuff and leave" I replied. She nodded her understanding and tucked her face in the crook of my neck. As soon as I felt rapid breathing against my skin I quickly moved through the room where her grandparents laid dead closing the door behind me. The smell of death was so violent in the air it sickened me. Don't get it twisted now ya'll know how I roll but this was not my doing. I would never have hurt my sister like this, so yeah it affected me.

We made it to her room, and I closed the door hoping to close out some of the smell, but it didn't work much. The stench seemed to have embedded itself everywhere. I put her on the floor and for the first time I was able to really look at her. She was beautiful, and she had eyes just like my ole' dude and myself. The thought of our lost plagued me. I was haunted in the worst way. The crazy part was I didn't know how to make it stop.

"Nem, where is your suitcase honey" I asked the little girl. She moved to the back of her closet and brought out a Dora suitcase and matching book bag.

"It's already packed" she whispered with her head down. The pain in her voice stabbed at my heart but I shook it off.

"Ok, let's go" I said while grabbing the suitcase and her hand. We existed the house as fast as we could. Even when fresh air hit my nose the smell of dead bodies lingered. As I closed the door behind me, I looked around. The sun was shining but the streets were deserted. It seemed as if no form of life existed. No one knew that a double murder occurred in the house where Nemis was raised. No one even gave a shit. Their lives will continue but this little girl's life will forever be altered no matter how much I try to shield her from the chaos.

Knowing that there was nothing I can do we walked casually to the car where I tucked Nemis in the back seat, securing her with the seatbelt and sticking her book bag and suitcase in the trunk. Once in the car I made a call to my father's cleaners and killers. They now worked for me. Calmly, I relayed the information for the cleanup sight. I told them what to do with the bodies and gave them the number of the funeral home to call for pick up. I also let them know that they were not allowed to leave until the bodies were picked up. I will bury them with my family to give my little sister a peace of mind. Even though I will not be staying in Detroit I will keep the cleaners on my pay roll. Their services will be greatly needed. First things first would be to bury my family and secure the safety of my daughter and sister. I looked at Nemis, her pretty eyes had unshed tears that fell when she made eye contact with me.

"I'm sorry Nem. I'm sorry I wasn't here to prevent this" I said softly. I then turned and pulled away from the only house that she has ever known, leaving behind her grandparents and her old life to start a new one that hopefully didn't involve her being exposed to senseless murders and sadness. She deserved better.

REVENGE IS MINE.... I thought to myself as I drove through the streets of Detroit. I looked at all the spots I have taken lives and thought maybe this is my punishment. But damn that, they violated when innocent people got hurt. I needed to get Nemis out of the city, but I had to stick around for a couple of days. My girls are all I have and that bothered me. They were motherless, and one is parentless completely, but she has me. It's a good thing that the estate was not breached. I can only guess that my parents were caught on the outside. I guess when my ole' dude realized that they were not going to make it out of the situation alive he sent out the already recorded email. Imagine my surprise after I listened to the email only to find out that my father was killed automatically. He was shot in the face. My mother on the other hand suffered a little. She was raped before they killed her. Luckily that wasn't thrown in my face because after seeing that shit with my wife I would have lost it completely. Back to the matter at hand technology is some amazing shit. Anyway, we can stay there until everything get settled.

It was going to be hard to be in a place where I grew up without the sound of my parents. I take my hat off to them though. They always prepared me for their deaths. So, even though it bothers me, I had plenty of time to get used to the idea. My wife on the other hand, is something totally different. My thoughts drifted to my baby girl. Pulling out my phone I placed the call to the only person I trust at this moment to secure the safety of my gift from my wife.

"Hello" a soft voice answered.

"Genesis, is my baby ok?" Getting straight to the point.

"She is ok Rocky. When are you coming back? She is getting stronger and starting to open her eyes, she is so beautiful."

"Thank you. I should be back in a few days. I'm not doing a complete service. Her family refuse to say their goodbyes. We have a family plot that they will be buried at."

Instantly, I started thinking about the plane ride back to Detroit. It was distracting knowing that my wife's body was just below mine. When I got off the plane and waited for everyone else to get off. Tears clouded my vision as the funeral home that was waiting pushed my wife's casket until they put it inside their hurse. With a shake of my head I got back to the conversation at hand.

"Ok well don't worry about Star I will be here for her every step of the way until you get back. Just do what you got to do and I'm so sorry for your loss."

"Thank you, Genesis, I really appreciate it. I will call you tomorrow" I responded.

"Your welcome. I will talk to you then" she said and hung up the phone. Just then Nemis blurted something out that damn near went over my head.

"Look out" she screamed.

I focused just in time to see a car coming straight at us like they were playing a game of chicken. With a sinister grin plaguing my face I kept driving until they swerved. When they did, I noticed a gun pointing dead at me. I instantly yelled "get down" to Nemis and made a quick left turn. The bullets shattered the back glass and I got pissed. As much as I wanted to turn around and do damage, I looked at the little girl in the back seat and decided against it. The car didn't pursue us which was a good thing. Rage on the other hand was burning my skin.

"You ok" I asked her.

"Yeah" she replied. She then paused and without even second guessing she blurted out "I'm hungry." I shook my head and realized she was not fazed by the bullets flying over her head. That wasn't good. I looked at her in the mirror and what I saw baffled me. Not only was she amused but a blur of rage was there. *Shit, she was going to have homicide tendencies if I don't get a hold of this shit.* Shaking my head, I kept driving letting her rage and amusement go for now.

"So am I. Let's go eat then. Is there anything particular you want" I asked the little girl knowing that I had to change the subject.

"Pancakes" she replied with a smile.

"Sounds good to me baby girl" I replied to her and continued to move through the streets looking for the nearest Ihop. I looked through the rearview mirror at Nemis again and I noticed a look of relief in her eyes. With a smile I turned my eyes back to the road and got lost in my thoughts. *Damn I got to get that fucking window fixed.*

Rocky

As you can see my life came crashing down on me and those I love. I never expected those racist to get the drop on my wife. I never thought that I will be burying her. To make matters worse she will never be able to hold our daughter, to see her grow, laugh or love. I know you probably think that I should just concentrate on these kids that I must raise, and you will be right, but scores must be settled. I just can't let this go. This wasn't no he stole my dog type shit. This was they took people I love away from me and mine. Granted, I would love to live in peace but at what cost? My little sister is still in danger and on top of that she seems to have the killer genes in her and if the members of Life for Whites find out that my wife and I had the baby she will no longer safe.

I hope you are not sitting there thinking that those fools are just gone let me get away with killing their kids. That will be silly of you. Personally, there is no way I'm going to let their kids get away with killing my wife even though they are dead. Nah, I want the whole organization to crash and every member of those boy's families to die by my hands. I don't kill kids but if they have some in their family that's corrupted, I may just have to take back that rule. They will be just like them if they are old enough to understand the hate. On top of that I still have a target on my back from both angles, but this isn't about me. I can take care of myself, but my princesses can't.

To be honest I even want to kill my wife's damn parents because those muthafuckas played my baby to the left when she needed them the most. So, at the end of the day fuck what everyone thinks. I'm gone end this shit once and for all when the opportunity presents itself. Hopefully, I don't loose myself in the process.

Anyway, after the pancakes, my little sister and I made our way to my parent's estate. I cannot explain the pain of being here. I showed her to the guest room that was next to mine and got her settled. She looked tired and believe me when I tell you that I understood that. These past couple of days for the both of us have been hell. As I watched her make her way to the bed, I couldn't do anything but recall our little conversation.

Come to find out she knew of me. Her favorite color is red, she likes dogs and wants one, likes to draw and spent plenty of time with our father. He also used to let her shoot a gun. Crazy right but the truth is ain't nothing wrong with preparation, but she shouldn't have to use what she was taught. On the other hand, that settled me a little

13

bit. It made me feel some type of way in a good way that she got to know the man that I love and respect. I gave her the PG13 version of my story and let her know that she has a niece that we must get back to. The conversation was pleasant, and it felt like we have known each other all along.

Anyway, once she was settled down for a nap, I stood outside my parent's bedroom door. I wanted to go in, but I couldn't. Hell, I couldn't even go in my room because the thoughts of my wife invaded my mind. Standing there in the hall contemplating, the down stairs couch sounded more of my speed. Once laying on the couch sleep took me under, and dreams invaded me.

I was in a room that looked like the warehouse I found her in. Chills ran down my spine, but I couldn't move. It was like I was frozen in place. Then she appeared. She was dressed in a beautiful gown, but her body was still bruised and battered. Dried blood still marred her skin and her long dreads. My heart broke at the sight of her. I was in the same clothes I committed those murders in. I felt like I had so much energy but mentally I was exhausted.

"Rocky…… Hey baby there you are. I hope you're not too mad at me for leaving you and the baby, but it was my time. Besides I left ya'll in capable hands." Her voice

sounded strained but there were no signs of pain on her face. Even looking beaten she still was so beautiful to me. I wanted her even in her state.

"Bliss…. Why are we here? Baby come back to us. My parents are dead, and I don't know what to do. I'm stressed. I miss you so much. I have Nemis and Star, I can't raise these girls alone. I need you…. Come back" I pleaded with my wife. She must see reason. She must know that her not being with me will not do any of us any good. She was my Rock. My own personal Bliss.

"I can't baby. My story has come to an end. Rocky, you will be fine with raising those girls and you're not alone. You don't have to do it by yourself."

"Baby what are you talking about? You're not here. Bliss please forgive me ma. I failed you. I let them get you. I will live with that regret for the rest of my life. But I am alone I must raise them alone ma without you. I need you Bliss."

Rocky…. I love you with my everything and you have someone to help you with those kids. You have someone who will give you what I couldn't. You must embrace and except what she has to offer you. You should see her for who she is and not just someone who helps you out. She was there when you needed her, and she is there

now for you and Star, which is a pretty name by the way.
She will be there for Nemis too. But a little advice my love
because I know you. You have a partner in crime. You met
him. At this point he will throw all rules out the window if
you reach out to him. Don't go up against those groups
alone this time. Reach out and embrace those who are
there for you. Plus, take some time and spend it with the
girls Rocky. They need a stable home. Get to know all of
them and move on baby because I can't come back. You
must love again Rocky for your sake and the sake of those
girls. This is the end of me…. I love you always and kiss
our daughter for me…. Bye my love.

Bliss…. I don't want to love another woman.
Blissss."

"Rocky" I heard a small whisper and I knew who it
came from, I just couldn't seem to open my eyes. I'm
confused. I have never been this apprehensive before. I
never felt like I had no control over myself. This shit was
unfamiliar, and I don't like it. I felt another small shake and
my eyes slowly climbed open and was met with eyes just
like mine.

"I couldn't sleep in that room all alone" Nemis said
looking at me with worrisome eyes. My heart stuttered. She
wasted no time climbing on the couch with me and

snuggling her little body close to mine. I pulled her closer because truthfully a hug was what I needed right now.

"I'm sorry Nemis I didn't mean to scare you" I responded. I heard the crack in my voice, and I knew I couldn't hold it in anymore. I cried for all that we lost. I couldn't see the light at the end of the tunnel. I only saw dark, and even though I alone welcomed it, but I wanted my babies to remain in the light.

"You didn't scare me Rocky. I know you hurt, so do I but we have each other, and we can go get the baby and be a family" Nemis said to me.

With a smile I replied, "Yes, we can Nem and yes, we will." I kissed her little head and we laid there comforting each other. Nemis's breathing slowed after a while and I got up from the couch walking towards my father's office. I glanced back at my sleeping princess making sure she was indeed in dream land. I needed to get this house in order, so I can sell it. I already been in contact with a realtor, so I just had to pack up the shit I was gone keep. Walking In, I looked around at everything noticing that nothing was out of place. I then moved towards my father's computer and logged on.

Instantly, I started searching for houses in the Lakewood Estates Subdivision located in Oconomowoc

Wisconsin. I always had a desire to go to Wisconsin out of all the places in the world. *That is where I want to settle my kids at. Truth be told if shit wouldn't have gone so sour, my wife and I was thinking about a relocation to Wisconsin once she had the baby and got done with school.*

Once I put a bid on a house that I thought will be fitting us I went to the garage to get some boxes. My pops always had those laying around for my mother. She was very much into donating clothes and other things.

Surprisingly there were plenty in there. Taking the boxes, I went back in the office and started boxing up things. I could have paid someone to do this for me, but this type of shit was keeping me busy. I was so enthralled with my chore that I didn't even hear my phone ringing. What I did hear was a soft voice whisper "hello." That's when I looked up and seen Nemis holding his phone to her ear, listening intently at whatever the caller was saying with a frown on her face. She handed me the phone and moved to sit in the chair that our father sat in so many times.

"Hello"

"Hi, Mr. Williams this is Ken from the funeral home calling. I was calling to inform you that we received the extra two bodies that you wanted prepped. In about four or five days all five bodies will be ready for viewing. We have contacted Bishop's Baptist Church and they are on board and will clear their schedule for the viewing at your convenience. We can call you when the bodies are ready if you will like? They will be transported to and from the church and to the grave site." Ken said.

"Yes, let me know as soon as you can so I can send out notices for the viewing. Thank you again. Add the extra two on to the final bill please."

"No problem Mr. Williams and I am truly sorry for your loss."

"Thank you" I replied then hung up the phone. Taking a deep breath, I turned towards Nemis.

"Looks like we have to go shopping kid."

"Are you going to bury my grandparents?"

"Yes, will that be okay with you?"

"Yes, there is no one else to do it. I don't know any other family members. Them and daddy was all I had" she stated as tears came about. I couldn't stand to see her hurting, so I went to her. I picked her up and held her while she cried her tears of loss. Life can't be this damn cruel. All this death we both were experiencing made me think about all the lives I took. I guess it's only fair. I did so much evil shit that my karma debt is a bitch. But, because of what has transpired I am only going to accumulate more and hopefully my princesses don't get caught in the cross fire. Abandoning those thoughts, I focused on Nemis.

"Nem, you have me and Star now okay" I whispered to her. "You're a big sister now and Star is going to need you to be brave and look after her. Can you do that for me?"

"Yes, I will look after our Star Rocky and you will look after both of us"

"Yes, baby girl I will. That's my promise to you. Now will you help me finish packing this office? Tomorrow we have to go shopping for clothes and maybe we will see something for Star." She nodded her head, kissed me on the cheek and wiggled so I will let her down. I did just that. She moved around the desk and started packing up the office. I followed suit and this time we both got lost in the chore.

By the time the office was packed it was around six in the evening. Nemis looked at me and smiled then looked around. Yeah, we made way, working together. I can already see she gone be my little helper.

"You hungry" I asked her. Nodding her head, she was walking towards the door. I frowned kind of confused by her actions but then she stopped and was holding herself. I understood then.

"The bathroom is over there Nem" I said pointing to the left side of the room. She sprinted there. Well, damn. Finding that I needed to relief myself I went to the guest bathroom down the hall. When I made it back to the office, she was sitting in the chair again.

"Okay so I want pizza" she said. Again, I nodded my head and proceeded to make the call. We went to the kitchen and stared at all the food that was in there.

"Well I guess we can box this Nem and donate it" I stated. She just smiled and started emptying out the closest cabinet she can reach. I started on the higher ones. *While doing that I thought about all the times I seen my mother move around this kitchen. In her zone and preparing food for her family. She loved to cook and was very good at it. She was the best. Of course, she may have made her mistakes, but I wouldn't trade her for the world. Now all I wanted was to hug her and enjoy a meal she prepared. Damn!* We weren't even half way finished by the time the buzzard rang. With the camera being there I just opened the outside gate letting the pizza man in. Grabbing my wallet off the table I met him at the door. Nemis was behind me at that time. *This damn girl moves to quietly.* We got the pizza and made it back to the kitchen. I grabbed sodas from the frig since there was no juice present. We sat at the table and

21

started eating out the box. We both was lost in our own thoughts. I was thinking about my wife, parents and my baby. I wanted to get back to her. My thoughts were about to take me into the danger zone, but a text came in on my phone. There was a picture message. Opening it my baby's face came into view, my eyes watered at her beauty. She was still hooked up to oxygen and shit, but her eyes were open and again they looked like mine. Her features though were her mother's all the way. Then a text message came through.

Genesis: She is such a beautiful girl.

Rocky: Yes, she is. Thank you for taking care of her for me.

Genesis: Anything for you Rocky. Have a good night. Talk to you tomorrow.

Rocky: Goodnight Gene.

I had to re-read the text messages again because I didn't understand what she meant about "anything for me." Shrugging my shoulders, I left that alone for another day and decided to show Nemis the picture of Star. She smiled her eyes lighting up. When I put the phone down no words needed to be said, we both went back to the emptying of cabinets.

By the time we got done it was around ten. I was beat and mentally drained, and I know Nemis felt the same way. She followed me upstairs to the bathroom where I ran her a bath.

"Do you need help Nem" I asked her. Praying and hoping she said no.

"No, I got it. Thank you though" she replied. Then she moved back towards the guest room and collected her night clothes and hygiene products. Smiling, I left the bathroom and went to my room. It smelled clean but images of Bliss lying on that bed under me invaded my thoughts. Shaking it off, I moved towards the shower and washed my ass thinking that I might crash on the damn couch. I know I needed to get over this shit but right now it's still fresh. Once done I put on pajamas and went to find Nemis. She was sitting on the bed in the guest room looking scared.

"What's wrong" I asked her.

"I don't want to sleep by myself Rocky. I had to in that panic room. I don't want to again" she said in a shaky voice. The fear so evident on her face. Knowing that I was going to have a panic room myself I still felt bad for her. I found blankets in the closet and grabbed her hand, we went back downstairs and snuggled up on the couch together.

Once settled sleep took both of us into our own separate dreams.

Genesis

I sat in the chair next to the incubator and watched Star sleep. I only seen her mother when she was hooked up to those machines, but I was able to tell that she was a beautiful woman. The creation between her and Rocky was amazing. Speaking of Rocky that man has been invading my thoughts ever since I saw him that awful night. I know it may be wrong, but I can't help it. My heart seems to soar at the thought of him. I never believed in love at first sight, but damn did I believe in it now. I know I should tread lightly considering he just lost his wife, and parents but damn not being with him is killing me. My world shifted when I laid eyes on him. What was important then seems to be secondary now. I just want to be in his world and apart of the lives that matter to him.

I have been in love before, but that shit was only one sided. Your probably confused right and I do remember telling you that I had a story to tell. I guess the time is right now.

I came from the slums of Puerto Rico and from a big family at that. We were a poor family. My parents worked their fingers to the bone everyday just to end up with pennies at the end of week. They worked seven days a week and still had to come home to deal with six children. I have five brothers. As you can tell being the only girl wasn't easy. I was picked on and bullied by my brothers, but they still looked out for me somewhat when my parents were there anyway. I didn't have many friends growing up and no boyfriends to boot. Yeah, my brothers and father weren't having that shit. Any who, as time went on and all my siblings and myself got older my mother got sick. Breast cancer took a hold of her and didn't want to let go. She stopped working and my brothers had to drop out of school to work. Bills had to be paid. The oldest three boys worked every day. They youngest two decided that they wanted to sell drugs to make money. They hooked up with the local street runners. I on the other hand was tasked with going to school during the day and taking care of my mother and myself at night.

The treatments my mom did get didn't work. The cancer spread fast, so it was too late for it to make a difference. I had to sit and watch my mother suffer. Pain itched her face daily and pain medication had got to the point where it was useless. My father didn't want to pay for a nurse to come in because that will take most of the house's income. The only thing I could do at that time was watch her wither away and eventually she died. I was ten years old.

Nothing changed as far as fending for me. When I turned sixteen my father died of a heart attack. That only left me and my brothers. They tried to do right by me, but they were so caught up in their own lives that I had no place in it. Eventually the brothers that was selling drugs ended up in prison. The other three worked and never got an education. They eventually found woman who didn't like that I was around much. They had to choose and of course since they forgot about me already, they chose their woman. At sixteen I was left alone.

The first born paid the bills at my parent's house but that was all. I had to figure out how I was going to eat. Sometimes I would eat so much at school that my stomach will hurt. Then, there were times where I stashed food in my locker to have for later in the day. Considering I was smart I graduated at seventeen. Once that source of food was gone, I had to think of other ways to eat. My clothes had gotten very small at that time. My situation was dire. So, one night I found myself on a corner where local prostitutes hung out at. It started out with simple hand jobs. I would jack off a couple of guys a night to get money for food and clothing. I always shopped at thrift stores.

27

One day a pimp came up to me and told me that working with him I can make a lot of money. Well, at seventeen that sounded good considering I didn't have a pot to piss in. He whined me and showed me how he will treat me if I worked with him. He was the one who took my virginity. I guess he had to break me in. Of course, I gave it to him willingly because I fell for him over the course of him whining and dinning me. I was a naïve seventeen-year old who thought this man was a hero and therefore was willing to do anything for him. His name was Marco. In my eyes, he was all I needed. I still stayed in my parent's house that eventually turned into my own personal fuck house. With my brothers being clueless, the older one still paid the bills.

Of course, I let Marco know what the deal was, and he respected that all activity had to seize during the day. That's when I slept anyway. Things were good for the first six months then all hell broke loose. Before I knew It, I was strung out on coke and Marco was beating my ass daily. I never saw any of the money I made. He made sure I had things like food and clothing. He even brought me a cheap ass car.

I was at my worse. I was a strung-out whore with an abusive boyfriend. Well, at least I thought he was. I lived that life for two years straight. I can't tell you how many men I slept with. I can't even tell you how many STD's I had. Luckily, it was never anything I couldn't get rid of. Luckily, it never made me infertile. My life was hell. Eventually my brother found out about my activities and stopped paying the bills. Marco took over but at a cost. I know had to fuck 24/7. Sometimes I went days without sleep.

One day after a beaten I had enough and figured death will be a better existence. So, I snorted a bunch of coke, drank a bunch of alcohol, even took some ecstasy pills he had laying around. When he found me, I was so out of it. Till this day I'm surprised my heart didn't stop beating. I guess the most highs had other plans. Anyway, I was in the hospital for a few days. This nurse that was treating me gave me a card of a church who helps fund relocation and housing for victims of domestic violence and drug abuse. Well, since I was that, I took it. When I left the hospital, I didn't use the card right away, but I kept it. I went to my house only found out that I didn't have a home to go to. Marco had set my parent's house on fire because he didn't want the cops snooping around. My almost suicide put them on his back.

I went to my brothers and asked for help, but they closed the doors in my face but not before telling me how much of a disappointment I was. Like they were the best to me. I spent a couple of days living on the streets then finally went to that church. They helped me get clean. Which was very fucking rough. After six months of detoxification they put me on the plane to Alabama and made sure I had a spot in a shelter until I found a job and got on my feet. By this time, I was determined to stay clean. I worked, got a little shitty ass apartment that was cheap and got a scholarship to attend Troy University School of Nursing and now here I am.

So, when I met Rocky all blooded up, his wife battered I knew in my heart that her state was not because of him. I knew in my heart that there was something dangerous about him and I should have let the cops handle it. But I couldn't, the broken look he had, broke my heart. I knew that at that moment I was going to do whatever I needed to do to help him. I knew I was going to be in his life one way or another.

Now you know my story. I have been in Alabama for almost five years. I never had a boyfriend here or even a lover. I don't have any kids and I'm in love with a man who just lost his wife and parents.

My life was shitty, but I am here. I picked myself up when someone gave me a chance and I made a better life for myself. I would never allow myself to get so low again. I don't even talk to my brothers, even though they have tried to reach out to me but what's the point. They weren't there when I needed them. Maybe one day I will but right now I don't need anything that will reminds me of my past. I only have my future to think about. I can only hope that my future involves the man I can't stop thinking about and the two little girls he is now responsible for. I can only hope that he will see that I have so much love to give. One day I hope to be his wife and give him more children. One day I hope he will let me be the support he needs.

Rocky

I felt my blood run cold as I stand here and watch my wife, parents and Nemis's grandparents get lowered into the ground. My heart seemed to have closed its doors on all except my girls. My body starts to shake, and my beast is trying to get free. He wants to destroy everything in his path. I am full of rage and at this point controlling it seems far-fetched. The beast was about to spring free until I felt Nemis put her little hand in mine. I calmed down at that moment, breathing deep, reeling in all the rage that was trying to consume me. I heard her sniffles and felt her tiny squeeze. Then, I heard people say their apologies for our lose but I didn't pay attention to them. I was concentrating on my sister now.

Once the bodies were seated where they were supposed to be, I looked across the grave yard and saw Ricky standing there. I gave him a curt nod, picked up my sister and left the place where our families lay to rest. At this time, I can only hope that I would step foot back in this graveyard and not in a casket. The moral of my story is I have unfinished business and all those who wronged me and mine will die.

The house was packed up and on the market. A check will be mailed to my location once it sells. The house in Wisconsin were just waiting on us. The things I kept from my parents were shipped besides the jewelry and the money which was deposited into my accounts and what I had on me. I already met with lawyers and insurance agents so there was nothing else for me in Detroit besides those I tend to kill later. I secured Nemis in the backseat and pulled out of the parking lot making my way to the airport. I refused the limo service that the funeral home tried to set up. I have one more place to pack and wait for my daughter to get strong, so we can get the fuck away from everyone for a while.

For now, I will put my murder spree on hold but only because my girls need me more at this moment. When we arrived at the airport, I turned in the rental and got our tickets.

"Rocky, I never been on a plane before" Nemis said.

"Nem, it's okay" I said impatiently as we moved through the airport and the crowd. I was in a foul mood. We were cutting it close, but we made it through security and to the gate just when they started boarding. We boarded first class of course and got settled. I put the shade down on the window so Nemis wouldn't look out of it. She looked scared but sat back in the seat and closed her eyes. The flight didn't take long to taxy down the runway. Before we know it, we were up in the air and her little hand was squeezing mine. I followed her lead and closed my eyes letting the feel of floating take me away. I wasn't sleepy, but my mental state was fragile and that alone was draining my energy.

I must have fallen asleep though because when I woke up the flight attendant was announcing our arriving in Alabama. Nemis was curled up in her seat with her head laying on my shoulders. I gently shook her awake and told her to sit up we were about to land.

Existing the plane wasn't much of a hassle but making it back to my truck was and let's not mention the damn traffic. I just wanted to change and go see my daughter. We arrived back at my condo and my heart started beating rapidly. There is no way I was going to be able to stay in this place. I called Staybridge Suites and made reservations for a two-bedroom suite while quietly showing Nemis where to change her clothes at. I went to the room and noticed the slight mess that was still in there. Shaking my head, I got in the shower and changed into some dark Levi jeans, a white beater, black t shirt, light

jacket and some all black air maxes. I packed a duffle bag
full of clothes, another with shoes and my hygiene
products. I went to the nursey and Nemis was standing in
there in some Limited Too blue jeans with butterflies on the
back pocket, pink Nike graphic t-shirt, jacket and some
pink and white pumas.

"Do you like the room Nem?"

"Yes, it's so pretty. Are we going to live here?"

"No, we are going to stay in a motel until Star is
strong enough to leave the hospital, then we are moving to
Wisconsin" I replied to her.

"Do we have to pack all this stuff up?"

"I'm thinking about getting someone to pack up the
baby's room but other than that the rest is going to get sold
or donated" I responded.

"Okay, can we go see the baby now? I can't wait to
meet her" she said with a pretty smile.

"I'll meet you by the door" I said then she moved
out the room. I walked back to my room and went to the
closet locating the safe back there that Bliss never made it
too. I took out one of my two babies and secured them on
me. I even grabbed Bliss's gun. Locking it back I made my
way through the condo and found Nemis standing at the
door waiting to go and meet Star. As I drove through the

streets of Alabama my mind was all over the place. I was thinking about nothing, but it seemed like I couldn't focus on one single thing. Focusing seemed to be something I couldn't do for whatever reason.

Walking through that hospital again was like walking into the pits of hell. The smell of death assaulted my senses making me want to gag. The feeling and memory behind this place weren't a good one but I have something good here to get to so that alone allowed me to keep walking through the halls. We boarded the elevator and made our way to the neonatal unit.

We made it to the window and Genesis was standing there holding Star and talking to her. My baby was cooing, and tears came to my eyes, but I didn't let them fall. There was something about Genesis. She has a big heart, she is caring and when I needed comfort she was there. Looking at her now I can see her in my future, but I can't really tell if it's something that I want to get to the bottom of intimately or if it's just a friendship type thing. One thing is for sure I can't analyze that right now. I have a goal and being in another relationship is not one of them.

"Hey" I said as Nemis and I stepped into the room. Genesis turned around with a smile on her face.

"Hey, look who is up and has been waiting on you" she replied. She looked down at the little girl that was holding my hand. "What's your name cutie" she asked.

"Nemis"

"That is a pretty name and unique" Genesis responded. I moved towards her with my hands out. This will be the first time that I get to hold my baby girl in my arms. This will be the first time I get to be so close to someone who reminded me of my Bliss. She placed her in my arms, and I moved to the rocking chair taking a seat.

Then I heard "thank you." I knew it wasn't my voice but everything else seems to be non-existent. My child was in my arms looking at me with familiar eyes, a beautiful face like her mothers. Then, at that moment I couldn't control the tears, they fell. My baby was a replica of the woman I love and lost. How will I ever be able to heal from this pain? Out the corner of my eye I notice Nemis moving closer to the rocking chair and her little hands swiped at the tears on my face.

"It's ok Rocky, don't cry" she said. Her voice was cracking with her own unshed tears. Genesis moved and pulled Nemis into her arms. We all sat there in happy tears mixed with sad ones but content. I looked at all the ladies in my life any realized that a nigga was lucky. I have a best friend and two beautiful girls. This is my life and I just happen to love it.

After the tearful event I feed Star, talked to her and we spent some time feeling each other out. Genesis took Nemis with her around the hospital to her patients. That concept was kind of crazy, but I do know that little kids have a way of making a sick adult happy, so I guess the whole evening was a "Nemis therapy event." Anyway, so when they came back in the room Star was in her incubator sleeping and I noticed it was around lunch time.

"Gene I'm going to take Nem to get something to eat. You can go do your work. The nurse here got it under control" I said

"Okay, sounds good" she replied and turned to walk out the room. I watched her walk away. I have been trying to figure out how she managed to keep Star in her sights and do her work all at the same time. To be honest I'm starting to think the woman was some sort of super hero. Don't get it twisted we all know I am not a weak ass nigga but being responsible for little people tend to make a nigga a little mushy. Damn!!!

"Gene, thank you for all your help. I really appreciate it." Her eyes seemed to glaze over and get hooded. That kind of through me for a loop but hey.

"Your welcome Rock" she replied then walked out the room for real this time. She added a little more switch in her hips. Yeah, I know I shouldn't have noticed but dammit I did. I noticed everything about her. From her curvaceous body to her dark complexion and her wavy hair. I am a man after all and yes, my dick did get a little excited, but I pushed the small amount of desire down, grabbed my sister's hand and we went in search of some damn food.

The whole reaction to her was crazy to me. My body was screaming for the closeness of Genesis, but my mind, body and heart was screaming for my wife. Yes, I get it my wife is dead but even though my body is ready to move on my heart and mind isn't so with my body don't run shit. Therefore, the desire is nothing and always will be nothing. I may eat them words somewhere down the line but at this moment and time that's how I feel. Besides Genesis deserves more than just having the dick laid to her. How do I know? Well, it's in her eyes. The eyes are windows to the soul and if you look hard enough you can see a person's true desires, wants, and needs. She needs an unconditional love type relationship. She needs everything that I gave my wife. I am not the one to give it to her because I am still unconditionally in love with my Bliss.

Ricky

I can't lie and say that I'm not hurting. I lost my sister and the woman I loved. Yeah you are probably confused about that. Well it seems like only I can explain it to you.

See Bliss and I grew up together just like her and my sister did. From the moment I laid eyes on that girl I wanted her. She was two years younger than me, but she seemed so old beyond her years. She always carried herself with respect and class. She was never in a nigga's faces like my sister and their other friend. Honestly it was her eyes that drew me to her. They were lost. You would think that a girl like her would always be happy. She came from a two-parent home, her family were Christians. Well, at least they pretended to be.

I think the lost look came from seeing her mother being treated badly. Her mother was never stood up for by her dad, he cheated on her, but her mother always told Bliss that is what woman do. They take whatever their husbands dish out to them. Bliss had to be confused by the situation. Over the years the lost look disappeared, and she developed a look of determination and confidence. I didn't know where the change came from, but I liked it. No, I loved it.   When she was sixteen, I expressed my love and interest in her. Granted, I was eighteen, but I knew what I wanted. She on the other hand didn't share those same feelings. So, to get away from the loss that I felt I went to the Navy. I spent years building myself and waiting for her to find herself. I thought I had time to convince her that she would be happy with me. Well, imagine my surprise when I found out I was too late. I was back way before my sister was murdered. At my sister's funeral I wanted express the love I had for her again but something in Rocky's eyes stopped me. I realized that even though I loved her and still do even in her death he needed her. The need he had was somewhat of a desperation. Even though she is dead believe me when I tell you that she saved his life, even though he couldn't save hers. Besides, I was not ready to die, and that man would have killed my ass. At that point though no one would have been able to save her life because the most highs already put the story in motion.

So, you see both of us is suffering at the loss of Bliss and I think that is why I have decided to give him my loyalty. I saw the look in his eyes at that funeral. I saw the way he looked at the little girl and all those coffins he was having placed in the ground. The beast in him is ready to take his revenge.

41

I knew that the baby was born so I made it my personal business when Rocky was going after the little girl to make sure that no one visited that baby. Again, my loyalty runs deep. He doesn't know that I have been watching those he cares about on the low. He doesn't know that I know who took out his parents and is searching for the little girl. He doesn't even know that I have been keeping tabs on the Life for Whites group. When the time is right all this information will be presented to him. I just must gain his trust first. I am doing this for Bliss. Her family is mine. I would have done anything for her, and I still will.

Speaking of my family I haven't had much to say to my parents after my sister's funeral. I was just baffled at how bad they treated Bliss. I was pissed at how her own parents refused to show up to her funeral. They think that her death was because of Rocky. What they don't know it was because Bliss stood up for what she thought was right, she would have died a lot sooner had it had not been for Rocky. I know about the bodies he left behind. I also know that he's going leave behind even more. I also know that the three ladies that is occupying his life is also his weaknesses. When the smoke clears, and all beefs are settled I would go back to the Navy and try to live out my own life. Hopefully to find my own wife.

Genesis

I noticed the looks Rocky have been giving me, but I don't think it meant what I wanted it to. I mean I know he sees me as a good friend, good person but I want him to see me as a woman. A woman that wants and desires him. I am a survivor. I know how to get down and dirty when I need to. Again, I know this may be wrong, but I sure can't help it. I want him, in every way that a woman wants a man. I want to give my body to him, heart, soul, more kids, hand in marriage. Look don't knock me ok.

Seeing his tears when he held Star pulled at my heart. I know it was because his wife wasn't there to share that experience with him. I also know it was because that was the first time, he held his child since she been born. I noticed how his little sister seemed to try and be strong for him, but she doesn't need to be. Rocky is being strong for the both and I am being strong for all three of them. I don't know how to get him to see that he has a family. I am willing to be a mother to both of those children. I am willing to be their support system that they desperately need.

Everything in me is telling me that he owns me in a good way. Yes, if you want to hear me say it, I am in love with him. I am willing to take on everything for him. But I guess I just must wait for him to come around.

Anyway, back to the matters of work. I go back to my floor and finish my rounds and my charting. The patients that did get to see Nemis was so happy to see a happy face. There is something about that little girl that makes people happy, even in her sense of turmoil. I concentrated on work for the rest of the evening and gave Rocky the space he needed to be with his girls.

I finished my shift and made my way home. A hot bath and some wine are in order. After my bath and my second glass of wine I sat down to watch some crap TV and eat some left-over food I had in the frig. My thoughts kept drifting back to Rocky and all he has been through. I know pain, anger, and pure rage. I have lived it and it kills me to see that he is currently living it. Not only that he has two other lives to take into consideration. No one knows what a person's trials are. He is battling with himself. He is stuck between doing right by those babies or giving himself what he really wants and that's to give in to that rage. I don't know what happened when Rocky brought his wife into the hospital that night. What I do know is when I looked in his eyes he wasn't there. A beast lives inside that man and it is pissed off.

Anyway, I turned off the TV and made my way to my bed. My body felt like it weighed a ton I was so tired. Tomorrow is a new day and hopefully progress can be made.

As soon as I closed my eyes the visions of that night came into view. *It was of Rocky in bloody clothes, and his wife wrapped in a blanket bloodied and bruised. His cat eyes hunted me and called to me on a deep level. I can't explain the pull in a dream. He was in pure emotional pain. His life will never be the same. In the dream I didn't approach him I just stood back and watched him from afar. Then it changed. The same battered woman appeared wearing a clean white dress. She had the prettiest smile on her face. She stood there looking me over then nodded her head in approval. I was stuck. I didn't know what to say or do. All I can do was look at her once beautiful face. Her eyes were sad even though a smile was on her face. Then she spoke to me.*

"He needs you" she said in a very soft tone.

"Why do you say that" I asked her confused.

"You are his forever. You are the one who has been chosen to heal him. He is broken right now Genesis and the only way he can heal is if you heal him."

"How do I do that? He doesn't show any interest in me that way. I know we are friends but on his end that is as far as it goes."

"Genesis, do you remember the look on his face when he brought me in? Do you remember trying to comfort him?"

"Yes, I remember."

"Well, that is the key. His comfort. You are the person he has been calling on. You are the person who can put his heart back together and help him raise those kids. Do you have feelings for him?"

"Yes, I do. They are very strong, and I feel so bad because he just lost so much."

"Don't feel bad things happened how it was supposed to Genesis. I was the starter, you are the one to finish. Insert yourself in the lives of those girls that will get him to look at you. Also, Rocky is going to fall emotionally because he has been holding in all his pain. When he does you just be there to catch him because that will be your way in full force. I know you probably think I am crazy by telling you how to attract my husband, but the truth is I want him to be happy even without me. I want him to love again as much as he loved me, maybe even harder. He deserves a good life. Him and those girls lost so much.

They deserve to be whole again. You, Genesis are the missing link. Don't disappoint otherwise I will haunt your ass." She said then disappeared.

I jumped up from my sleep breathing hard and shocked. I can't believe a ghost from my dreams just threatened me. It's shocking because it seemed so real. I looked at the clock and it read just a little bit after two in the morning. I picked up my phone to text Rocky.

Genesis: Are you awake?

Rocky: Yes, what's up?

Genesis: I was just thinking about you. Why are you up?

Rocky: Nemis had a nightmare and I just got her back to sleep. Also, sleeps seem to evade me, so I deal with it.

Genesis: Is there anything I can do to help you sleep?

Rocky: Nah, I'm good. I will go eventually.

Genesis: Where is Nemis right now?

Rocky: Laying here next to me. We are at a motel. I had my condo cleaned out today.

Genesis: You guys could stay with me.

Rocky: Thank you Gene but I will have to decline that offer.

Genesis: Rocky come on. We are friends. It's going to be another couple of weeks before Star can leave the hospital and I know you plan on leaving town, but I want to help you. Please, let me help you Rocky. I can help you with Nemis. I am thinking about taking a vacation since I haven't taken one in a couple of years. I have all this time saved up. Let me take the time and help you until you leave. There is no need to stay at a motel when you have me.

Rocky: I can always use the help with Nemis, I don't know anything about taking care of a kid, but I can't move in with you Genesis. Besides you seem to be pretty good with kids.

Genesis: So, are you saying that I automatically have a mothering gene?

Rocky: Yeah, something like that I have heard about how you cared for Star while I was gone. I really appreciate that by the way.

Genesis: You're welcome. You will learn how to take care of them but yes, you have me to help you. So how about I take Nemis off your hands for a couple hours tomorrow since it is my day off so you can go and spend some time with Star. I want to take her to the zoo.

Rocky: That will be nice. She can use some fun. Baby girl has been through a lot and a joyful time will do her some good.

Genesis: Ok, so it's a plan.

Rocky: Thank you Genesis

Genesis: Your welcome

Rocky: Good night

Genesis: Good night baby.

With that I put the phone down without touching any buttons, at least I thought I did. I laid down and closed my eyes. Images of him naked popped into my head and I felt my pussy clench. I sat up and removed my clothes then laid back down. Still thinking about how big his dick may be and the feel of his fingers and tongue on my wet needy core I pinched my nipples. A gasp escaped my lips and one hand ventured down to my most intimate place. I rubbed my fingers over my hard clit and sensations that I haven't felt in a long time ran through me. I had to see what it felt like to finger myself with the thoughts of my Rocky. I buried two fingers into my tight wet pussy and fucked myself while playing with my nipples. I felt a quiver in my stomach and then my body released its built-up tension.

"Rockyyy" I called out then fell asleep.

Rocky

I moved off the bed when Genesis's number appeared on my caller ID. But I was stunned when I heard moans of pleasure through the phone speakers. My dick got hard and I had to dash to the bathroom. Pulling my dick out I stroked it hard and fast. Her moans increased and so did my speed. I worked hard to keep my moans silent, but my breathing increased. I was close. Then I heard her call my name, cum shot out of my dick all over the toilet seat. Her breathing slowed then it got quiet. I hung up the phone, cleaned up my mess and made it back to the bed. I moved Nemis over and laid down staring up at the ceiling. Something isn't right.

My thoughts drifted to Genesis. Her walk was sassy, the way she flips her long wavy hair is sexy, the color of her skin was beautiful, and her eyes talked to me all the time. I didn't know if I was able to keep being friendly with her, but I knew I was confused about what it was that I was feeling. As much as I called for my wife it seems like body was betraying me and her. My body wanted Genesis. I wanted to feel how tight her pussy would be on my dick. Hell, I want to watch it go in and out. I felt guilty. I feel like I'm cheating on my wife. Damn, how confused was I?

I decided that whatever I wanted didn't matter. These girls needed a good woman in their lives even if I couldn't have one. So, putting my desires on hold, I turned over and looked at my little sister's back until blackness pulled me under.

When I woke it, I felt like someone was staring at me. I turned my head to my left and Nemis was looking at me like she was mad.

"What's wrong girl" I asked in a groggy voice.

"You took all the covers" she said. Her little forehead crinkled, and it took everything not to laugh. This girl was a trip. She reminded me of my dad so much.

"Nem, I'm sorry I was tired" I said and the wrinkles in her forehead disappeared. "Do you forgive me" I asked.

"Only if you get up and feed me" she said aggressively. Shaking my head, I looked at the clock on the side table. Ten in the morning. Damn I overslept. I sat up on the side of the bed and looked at Nemis. She was dressed in some dark Levi jeans, a flannel long sleeve shirt and some white Nikes. Yeah, she was my father's child alright. I remember being independent at her age to. I refused to let my mother do anything for me. Well, besides iron my clothes.

"Did you iron your own clothes Nem" I asked her confused. She was dipped out with no wrinkles in sight.

"No, my grandma did before she packed my bag. All my clothes are like this." She said dropping her head.

"Hey, don't cry. I'm sorry for asking."

"I'm not going to cry Rocky I just get sad because they died because of me and so did daddy." She said. I pulled her to me and hugged her.

"Nem, they died protecting you just like daddy. You did nothing wrong and they wouldn't want you to be sad. They would want you to be happy. It's okay to think about them but don't let it make you sad. They love you Nem." I said to her. She smiled at me and my heart skipped a beat. Both of those girls will be the death of me one day, but I will have it no other way. "Now let me get myself together so we can go eat, besides Genesis wants to spend the day with you."

"I like her Rocky. She will make a good mommy for me and Star" she said looking at the TV. I looked at her and let that thought set in, then, I dismissed it. Turning, I made my way to the bathroom taking my bags with me and the sounds of SpongeBob in my ears. *That damn sponges laugh is irritating ass fuck.*

By the time I made it to the address that Genesis sent to me it was almost 2pm. I guess this is the perfect time for them to venture to the zoo. Breakfast and Lunch was already taken care of. I pulled up in the parking lot, parked the car. Taking a deep breath Nemis and I exited the car. I grabbed her hand and made my way to the apartment that Genesis resided in.

Her apartment wasn't in a good neighborhood, but it wasn't that bad either. I had a small 22 caliber gun in my glove box that I took out the gun safe the other day. Well, it looks like it's about to go to Genesis now. She was going to have my sister with her so I had to make sure she can protect her.

Anyway, her apartments were the kind that was side by side, which in my book was great especially when small kids were involved. I arrived at her door and she opened it. It was like she was looking out the window or something. With a smile she moved out the way and I was stunned. Her apartment even though it was a one bedroom was not small. The living room was very spacious. There was a small eating area and the kitchen was off to the side and had a decent size to it. She had chocolate colored furniture

54

that complimented the colors she chose to decorate the apartment in.

"Let me give you guys a tour" she said in a sweet tone. I locked eyes with her, and the sound of her moans rang in my ear.

"Damn! I mean okay" I said. She smiled and looked at Nemis who was staring at me like she knew my secret. I shook my head at her.

"Hi, Nemis" Genesis said to her and pulled her to her for a hug. Nemis went willingly, still with that damn secret look on her face.

"Hi Genesis" she said with a smile. Her eyes shined with pure amusement. Genesis stood and turned to give us the tour. My eyes went straight to her ass. It was very plump and looked soft ass fuck. I can't lie I wanted to fuck her and bad. I didn't know if it was because she was being nice, I was confused, or I just needed to fuck and relief some stress before my rage got the best of me. She gave us a tour. Just like the rest of the house it was tastefully decorated, spacious and clean.

"Look I'm going to let yall get going and I will see yall later" I said walking towards the door. I got there and turned around to see both looking at me like I was crazy.

"What?"

"Nothing" they replied in unison.

"Nem, give me a hug" I said to the little girl. She smiled and made her way to me. I hugged her and kissed the side of her head.

"See you later Rocky" she said pulling away from me. Then, I noticed that her hair was not done. It was long and I felt kind of ashamed that I didn't pay attention to that. She is so independent I thought she knew how to do that too. This comes to show you I know nothing about kids.

"Um, Gene her hair" I said to her. She giggled at me.

"I got it Rocky" she responded.

"Can you come outside for a minute I have to give you something." She said nothing and just followed me. I turned my gaze to Nemis, and she nodded her head. Once outside and at the car I pulled the small gun out my glove box and put it in her hand. She looked at me with shocked eyes.

"You know how to use that don't you" I asked huskily. She just nodded her head.

"Keep that on you at all time Gene okay."

"Why?"

"My wife's death wasn't an accident Gene. But to move on from that I need to know that while you have

Nemis you can protect her." She looked at me with tears in her eyes and it dawned on me. I just made her feel like I didn't care about her safety.

"Look, don't cry I didn't mean it that way. I care about your safety to, but she has a target on her back Gene. I need her safe. Do you understand that. I don't want to lock her up away from the world. She has been through so much and time out will do her some good" I said to her.

"I know and I'm sorry."

"You have nothing to be sorry for. Just be careful and vigilant. Follow your instincts. If you have any weird feelings, then you get yourself and Nemis to me no questions asked" I told her. She just nodded her head in understanding. I then, pulled out my wallet and gave her a wade of cash.

"What is this for? Rocky I don't want your money" she said angry now. I just smiled at her.

"I know you don't but yall enjoy yall selves on me. Let me do this. Do what girls do and I will see yall later." With that I walked her back to the apartment door and once she was inside with Nemis I turned and made my way towards my truck. I will go see my daughter. Then, Ricky and I need to have a conversation. He has some fucking explaining to do.

Ricky

I was surprised when I received a call from Rocky asking me to meet him at his condo. That was an odd place to meet but I went. Once inside the look he gave me chilled me to my bones and I realized that maybe I should have met him in public. Scared of course not but cautious, hell yes.

"What's up" I asked and crossed my arms across my chest.

"Why the fuck does you have people watching me. I noticed them at the hospital, my motel, at Genesis's and following me. Dude you have two fucking minutes to explain otherwise you are going to die in this damn place."

"Rocky calm down damn. I put a detail on all of you for your safety not for anything else. Word around is Life for Whites have been looking for you. They want blood for those boy's death."

"I don't give a fuck Rick."

"You have those girls Rock. They deserve to live."

"Are you implying that I can't protect my damn kids." I said in a low dangerous tone taking a step towards him. His body language never changed.

"No, I'm not implying that Rocky. I'm just saying that I want to help you protect your kids and the woman."

"Why?"

"Man, I loved Bliss to Rocky. She was the love of my life, but you were the love of hers. Why not offer my hand to help? Besides she was innocent and lost her life. Your child lost her mother and you lost your wife and parents. That must be a hard pill to swallow. I can only imagine that you have some built up anger that you haven't expressed yet. I know you want blood. Shit I don't blame you. Just let me help you man. No, strings I just want to help." I said. Rocky sighed.

"Man, I am angry. But I can't afford to lose it. Those girls depend on me." He replied.

"You know that woman is in love with you right?"

"I can't think about that right now. I am in love with my wife." He said in a low tone. For a while we just stood there both looking at the floor. We moved towards the door and made our exit at the same time.

"I'll be in touch. I may have some information for you. Just promise me that I get to go and kill with you" I said with a serious look on my face. He just nodded his agreement and we both left the condo. I on the other hand made a call.

"Do you have the location of the organization yet Blaze"

"Not yet sir, but they have been busy. They haven't located them yet though.

"And they won't. Rocky is no slouch, and this is not his first dance. He knows how to get lost. Just get me that information so we can put an end to this shit" I said then hung up the phone.

I just drove around letting my thoughts take me. The vibe coming off that man was dangerous and if he doesn't get a hold on it, he will explode. Not thinking about him too much I called a woman that I have been fucking since I been home. I met her at this grill and bar. She was no Bliss, but she was a nice piece of ass. Besides, if I don't bust a nut soon, I am going to explode.

"Hey, babe" she cooed.

"I'm on my way" I said and hung up the phone.

Rocky

I noticed the guys Ricky put on me the moment Nemis and I touched down. I just choose to ignore them at first but now they were getting on my damn nerves. I intended on beating the shit out of him when I called him to my old condo but the look in his eyes when he explained his actions to me gave me a moment to rethink that idea. He loved my wife. Funny, but I knew that when I met him at Levi and Remy's funeral. She told me I can trust him and from the looks of it she was right.

When I left him my thoughts drifted to Star? Spending the afternoon with her was heaven. She is so much like her mother already. So damn demanding. Those girls don't understand that they have me wrapped around their little fingers. They rule me and I rule nothing ain't that something.

Before I knew it, I made it back to Genesis's apartment. I got out and walked to the door I paused trying to hear what was going on, but it was quiet. I looked towards the parking and noticed that her car was there. Looking at my watch it read 9 pm. I had been gone all day. I spent so many hours with Star that time just flew by. The talk with Ricky didn't take long.

Anyway, I tapped on the door and waited for her to open it. She did it in a hurry. I took in the scene and noticed that Nemis was on the couch sleep.

"How was your day?" She asked.

"Beautiful, I guess I lost track of time. Was she good for you?" I asked pointing at Nemis. She smiled again.

"Yeah she was good. We went to the zoo, shopping and got clothes, out to eat. We had a ball all on your expense." She said grinning. I nodded and grinned myself.

"That's what's up. Look we need to get out of here"

"Yall can at least stay the night Rocky"

"Thanks Gene but that's not a good idea" I said as I walked over to Nemis and scooped her up in my arms. I kissed Genesis on the forehead then walked out. My body was on fire.

We made it back to the Motel in record time and before I knew it, I had Nemis tucked away in the second room and myself in the shower with thoughts of a sexy ass woman in my head. My dick was hard, and I was uneasy. Not because I wanted her but because something was about to go down and I wasn't sure I was ready for it. I always stayed on my shit but having distractions that came in the form of little people kind of put a person off balance just a little bit. I was trying so hard to be in tune with them and not let my constant aggression show but my beast was getting very fucking impatient. He never screamed at me this much to be let loose. So, to distract him I started jacking my dick with the thought of my wife in my head this time.

Once done with my internal struggle that happened in the bathroom I went to my bed and stretched out. I never realized how tired my body was until it hit that bed and my eyes seemed to close involuntary.

"Rocky"

"Yes Nem" I said still with my eyes closed.

"Can I sleep with you again" she asked. I signed but then tapped the other side of the bed. She instantly climbed on and cuddled close to me.

"Will it be okay if I call you daddy and Star my little sister" she asked

"If that is what you want to do Nem but understand I am your brother baby girl"

"I know. I just want a daddy" she said to me as her voice cracked. My heart squeezed.

"Nemis, baby girl you can call me daddy. Don't cry."

"Okay daddy. I love you" she said to me. *Yeah me and my babies will be just fine.*

"I love you to Nem, now go to sleep" I said to her. She relaxed in my arms and her breathing slowed. I closed my eyes and let my blissings take over me.

The next morning, I woke up to some damn paw patrol and the buzzing of my phone. I signed and shook my head. *This shit is going to take some getting used too.* I didn't know which one was more irritating. I looked at the phone and noticed a text from Ricky

Ricky: Wake your ass up!

Rocky: You got some information for me.

Ricky: Yes, and no. I don't know the location of their organization, but I do have eyes on a few members who have been strolling the streets looking for you.

Rocky: Where

Ricky: Well, considering your condo has not sold yet they have been casing it day and night after we met there.

Rocky: Send me the information I need a relief

Ricky: I want in

Rocky: Fine Ricky. Tonight. Pick me up at the Staybridge Suites at 9pm. Dress in all black those are my signature colors.

Ricky: Alright I'll see you then.

I sent Genesis a quick text letting her know that I needed her at 9pm and texted her the address to the Suites we stayed in. She replied with a quick ok. I looked at Nemis and knew from the look she gave back to me that I needed to move my ass.

Genesis

I can't begin to explain to you how hurt my feelings are. I really wanted Rocky to stay with me last night. He keeps rejecting me and I'm starting to wonder if it will always be like this. I know he isn't doing it on purpose. I also understand his reasoning. I just wish he will give in to me. I just wish that he will give me just a piece of him then at least I can be patient for the rest. That kiss he landed on my forehead was innocent I know but I couldn't help but to get excited about it. My panties grew wet and nipples got hard. My body tended to have a mind of its own whenever he is around, or my thoughts drifted to him. My heart called for something that might not ever happen and it was fucking frustrating.

Anyway, the text I received this morning sent a shiver up my spine. Even though it was a simple address and time I knew there was a meaning behind it, and it had nothing to do with us. The aura around him let's me know who he really is. He is a dangerous man, but I got the feeling that he is no danger to me or the girls. He harms those that deserve it. Well, at this point anyway. My loyalty to him is real, if only I can get him to see that. If only I can tell him that his wife wants us together. That his wife wants me to help him raise those girls and heal them all. She thinks I'm the key to their happiness, but he thinks I'm the key to his disloyalty to her. That concept is mind blowing.

Once Nemis and Rocky left I felt alone. I know that he has no intention on coming back here. I decided that I will not sit around and mope. Granted my heart is hurting from his rejection, but I refuse to lose myself again for a man. I will try to move on from him and maybe he will see what he is missing.

I showered and got ready to work. More than likely I will see them at the hospital visiting Star. I won't intrude. I will go and see about the baby then give him his space. I will see them again tonight though.

Once at work things were in total chaos. Code blues were being called. The emergency room was piling up and from the looks of it plenty of admissions was going to be made. Taking a deep breath, I dived into my work and lost myself in it. Before I knew it, it was shift change and I didn't go and see the baby. I gave the oncoming nurses the information they needed on the patients and made my way to the neonatal unit. I walked in and was shocked at how baby Star was filling out. She was getting healthier and stronger by the day and soon she will be at home with her daddy and sister. I kissed the baby on the forehead, looked at my watch and dashed out the door. I also took out my phone and seen a text message from Rocky with room number. I made it to my car without too much trouble and weaved through traffic. I don't want him to think I am unreliable.

By the time I made it to the Suites he was living in I had ten minutes to spare. I knocked on the door and this fine man with a fresh haircut, fresh facial trim, and dressed in all black opened the door. His aura screamed at me. The look in his eyes let me know that he indeed had an alter ego and he was about to be let loose. I got a feeling that something bad was going to happen and I was powerless to stop it. He moved out the way and I walked in. I noticed two separate bedrooms as I walked through the suite.

"Thank you for watching her for me Genesis" he said low and huskily. *Damn.*

"No problem. Where are you going" I asked and turned towards him. He stood there and said nothing. Then he cocked his head to the side and still said nothing. "Please be careful Rock. We need you" I stated by mistake. I meant to say the kids. His eyes glazed over, and he took a step towards me. His energy was heavy and angry. I felt it. I never moved away from him though.

"I'll be back. Nemis is in her room laying down. She's mad at me because we didn't return to your place today" he said then turned and walked away and out of the suite.

I walked to the bedroom that Nemis was in and looked at the pretty little girl with the cat eyes. She turned her head towards me and ran too me. Her hair was done too. Tiny little French braids adored her small head. They were going up into a pony tail.

"Wanna watch a movie with me?" she asked hopeful.

"Of course, what are we watching" I said kicking off my shoes.

"Boss Baby. I never seen it" she said again and moved to the bed.

"Where are the snacks?" I asked with a smile on my face.

"He told me he didn't want me to have too much sugar, but he brought animal cracker and popcorn" she replied.

"How about both with some milk"

"Yeah!!"

I collected the items then we got back in the room to watch the movie. I would have to say that is was good and funny. After the movie Nemis looked at me sadly. It hurt my heart.

"What's wrong baby girl"

"Rocky is hurting"

"I know baby, but he will be okay. He has you and Star"

"Does he have you Genesis?" she asked.

"Yes, honey he does" I responded.

"I never had a mommy Genesis and Star lost hers. All we have is our daddy" she said sadly. I pulled her to me and wrapped her in my arms.

"You guys have me to Nem. I promise" I said and rocked the little girl. Before I knew it, she was asleep.

I laid her down in the bed and made sure she was tucked in tight. I thought about the promise I made, and I realized that I intended to keep it. There will be no getting rid of me. I am here to stay. I made my way to the couch in the living and had to look around. This suite was nice as hell. I then decided to give myself a tour and when I walked in the room that Rocky sleeps in the scent of him engulfed me. My pussy instantly got wet and I knew that if I didn't get out of his room fast, I was going to strip naked, lay in his bed and finger fuck myself blind. My body called to him, but it also called to reason. He doesn't want me.

That concept brought tears to my eyes, but I blinked them back. On the flip side I thought *what the hell.* I striped out of my scrubs and took a hot shower. I used my hand lotion in my purse to lotion up my body. Once done with that I laid on his bed and realized he haven't laid on the sheets yet because they have been changed. The scent was just in the air. That didn't deter me though I closed my eyes and let my imagination take over. Seeing him looming over me with that blazed over look made my nipples pucker up. I ran my fingers over them, pinched them and let my imagination take me so deep into my fantasy that I didn't hear his bedroom door open.

Rocky

I sat in this car with Ricky pissed off. The racists that he said have been casing my condo was knocking on the door thinking they were going to catch me off guard. My mind went to my wife and her battered body clouded my vision. Tears formed but I let my beast out of the cage, and he was not in the mood to cry. He wanted blood. He wanted all those muthafuckas to die.

My body tingled and my dick hardened, and Ricky looked at me like I was crazy. I ignored him as I bobbed my head and my beast growled. That has never happened, but he was angry and excited. I turned and looked at Ricky, as he met my eyes a flash of fear crossed his face before it disappeared. I turned my head from him to see the car driving off.

"Follow" I said, and he obeyed still without saying a word. I took the liberty to put my silencers on my babies, so no one can hear. When they got to a dark street and stopped at a red light, I jumped out the car before Ricky can stop me and let off some rounds at the lowered windows. I never miss. Once I lowered the guns four member in that car all had bullet holes in their bodies. I never said anything I just got back in the car and Ricky followed my lead. My body was screaming at me and I knew I needed to get to a bathroom. Still I sat there breathing hard with my head laid back and my eyes closed.

When I looked up again Ricky was pulling up to my motel.

"I need the location Ricky" I said in a husky voice. Again, he said nothing but just looked at me for a minute. I then turned my head towards him, and his brow creased.

"What" I asked

"Are you ok" he asked me in return. I grinned and shook my head.

"Yes, why"

"Just worried about you man. You looked almost evil" he rebutted back. I bust out laughing. Shit if only he knew. I just answered him with a shake of my head and existed the car. I made my way through the motel on auto piolet. My body still carried on its state, but I was vigilant.

When I entered the suite, it was quit. I walked towards Nemis's room to check on her and she was sleeping peacefully. I looked at her and thought of my father. If only he knew how strong she really was. I kissed her little forehead then made my way out closing the door behind me. I then walked towards my room. The door was cracked but I heard soft moaning coming from there. I creased my brow and made a silent promise that if Genesis was in there fucking somebody, I was going to fucking kill them both. That promise kind of bothered me, but I pushed it back. What greeted me instead was the beautiful sight of a golden-brown body lying on my bed, legs opened wide, eyes closed, and two fingers plunging in and out of her shaved pussy. Her scent was intoxicating, and my body was still in need of a relief. I watched for a minute as I silently closed the bedroom door. Before long I couldn't take it anymore. I had to have her. I striped off my clothes as quietly as I can and moved towards the bed. My dick was pointing straight at her.

She must have felt the bed dip because she opened her eyes and looked directly at me. She saw what I needed. She pulled her wet fingers out of her pussy and held her hand out to me. My beast latched on to her fingers and sucked her juices off. Her hips involuntary arched up and I moved her fingers out of my mouth and latched on to her clit. I sucked her bud hard and hungrily, licking her viciously. She moaned my name and grabbed the back of my head. *Damn she tasted so good.* Even though I wanted to taste her cum my dick needed to be buried.

In a haste, at that moment I needed to be inside of her. Without thinking I moved up her body and buried my dick deep in her. She screamed out from the pain and that's when I noticed how tight she was.

"I'm sorry baby I just need you so much right now. The next time I'll take my time" I said in soft tone but a husky one. She said nothing but planted her sweet lips on mine. I instantly deepened the kiss and started fucking her hard and fast. She clung to me, her pussy clung to me and I was in deep ecstasy. *I haven't felt this good in a while.* As I fucked her and sucked on her tongue, she started bucking her hips at me. Meeting me thrust by thrust.

"Of fuck Rocky. Please baby fuck me harder please." She begged after she broke the kiss. I felt her pussy clench against me again. Her body started to shake. It was then that I noticed how bad she wanted and needed this to. I pounded her relentlessly as her orgasm overtook her body and I felt squirts coat me while thick cream stuck to me. I didn't stop though. I turned her over to lay her on her stomach. I rammed my way back in her sweet, wet pussy and started fucking her hard again. I was an animal in heat. Nothing could come in between this moment. She exploded again and this time mines followed. I knew I should have pulled out but my need to claim her took over, so I let my cum spray her walls, marking her as mine. The alpha in me was satisfied but the logical part of me was pissed off.

I figured that I should just enjoy this so that's what I did. I pulled out of her and pulled her to me. Tonight, she was my comfort and I was going to hang on to it until morning anyway. Besides, who said that I couldn't fuck her. That don't mean I have to love her right? I know you probably think I'm an asshole and technically you will be right but that don't mean that I give a fuck about that either. Without thinking I closed my eyes and let sleep take me and the smile of my wife came into view.

"I'm proud of you Rocky. I'm proud that you are letting good people near you and the girls" she said

"What are you talking about Bliss" I asked

"Genesis, Ricky"

"Ricky is cool, but Genesis is just a friend Bliss" I said to her and her smile disappeared.

"Did you use her Rocky because of the state you were in" she asks and growled. I have never seen her so angry.

"I don't know" I responded. She then looked at me with so much disappointment it brought me to my knees.

"I will not come to you I your dreams again until you understand what I am placing in front of you." She said then disappeared and I never got a chance to respond.

I opened my eyes and turned my head, Genesis was looking at me. Tears finally ran down at the pain of my wife abandoning me. The pain of losing her now for good. The dreams kept me grounded but I managed to lose that.

"What's wrong" Genesis asked in a concerned tone.

"She left me Gene" I said.

She wrapped her arms around me, and I cried like a damn baby in her chest. If you are wandering no I don't feel any less of a man because the truth of the matter is a real man have no problem crying when he is hurting especially after everything I have been through. But what is shocking is this woman that I just deposited my seed in held me and didn't let go at all. She didn't abandon me. Don't get me wrong I do understand that my wife is dead, but Genesis wasn't. So still even though I feel how I feel why do I still feel like I'm cheating on my wife. The wife who has left me in so many ways. After the tears dried up. I looked up at Genesis and she smiled at me. I took that as she thought nothing about me crying either and buried my face back in her chest and let sleep take me again. This time I was greeted with pure darkness and I found a much-needed peace there.

Genesis

I knew when he fell asleep. His breathing became even but deep. His body still but his face stayed buried in my chest. My heart swelled but I knew I had to be ready for anything. Even though I had a feeling that he might reject me the next morning I still couldn't find it in my heart to feel bad about what we did. He is after all the only man that I have been intimate with. He is after all the only man that I have wanted in the last five years. How do you explain your past to someone when they won't even let you be a part of their future?

I know he cares about me but is he capable of loving me like he loved his wife? Is he able to see that I am what he and those girls need like his wife sees? I'm confused about this whole thing. Even though I am so glad that I finally got to experience him I still don't know where I stand and that still leaves me apprehensive. But for tonight I am going to enjoy the feel of him in my arms and see what tomorrow brings.

As I closed my eyes, I saw nothing but light. I didn't follow it I just looked at it. By the time the light disappeared I was opening my eyes to meet cat like eyes, a five-o clock shadow and a sexy man.

"How did you sleep" he asked in a whispered tone

"Fine"

"We should talk about last night"

"Let's not. How about we just enjoy what we did together and call it that"

"Genesis, I don't want you to get the wrong idea. I was in a very highly sensitive state last night and I couldn't see beyond what my body was going through. I'm sorry I took advantage of you" he said. That pissed me off and broke my heart. I said nothing I just got out of bed hiding my face from him. I didn't want him to see me cry and I knew that if I turned to look at him that was going to happen. I hurried and put on my clothes. I had to get out of here. I know I was expecting this, but it doesn't make it any easier. I know he will never love me, but it just dawned on me that I needed to get over it. I will always be here for those girls, but I can't allow a man to keep hurting me.

"Genesis, please talk to me. Don't just walk out" he said. His voice was low and sad. I spared him no look.

"Where is Nemis"

"She's still sleeping" he responded back.

"Tell her I will call her later." I then left the room, collected my things and walked out the door without looking back at him. It felt like my heart just exploded in my chest. I mean seriously what do I have to do for this man to understand how much I love and want him and those girls? He said he took advantage of me and honestly, I didn't feel like he did until he said that shit.

I made it to my car, and I couldn't hold back my tears any longer. I broke down and cried my heart out. It already felt like it fell out of my chest. By the time I collected myself I was no longer in a crying mood. I was in a pissed off mood. I decided that I was going turn my phone off, clean my apartment and have a day with just me. A person gets tired of given and never getting in return.

When I got home, I instantly turned off the phone. I collected everything I needed to clean and set out to do just that. Once done with that I went to this Italian restaurant close to me and ordered me some food, stopped by the store got some wine and made it back home in time enough to enjoy a hot bath and watch crap TV.

By the time I pulled myself from in front of the TV it was eight at night. The day went fast but that's ok. Tomorrow I go back to work, and I can drown myself in that too. I then picked up my phone and turned it on to see who called. I had five missed calls come through, five text messages and a voicemail. Three of those calls was from Rocky, all the texts were from Rocky and the voicemail was from my job. I ignored all of them and took my ass to bed for a busy and hard day tomorrow.

By the time I made it to work the next day I was in a very foul mood. I had damn near ran out of gas. Then, I caught a fucking flat tire. It's a good thing I knew how to change one. I didn't waste any time though. I made my way through my rounds. It wasn't until I even walked inside Star's room that I even noticed that I was on the neonatal unit floor. I have been in auto piolet all day. I walked in the room and saw Nemis sitting in the chair holding Star. Rocky was standing nearby and looking down at the duo. Nemis noticed me first.

"Hi, Genesis" she said in an excited voice.

"Hi, honey I see your holding the baby"

"Yeah, she is getting so big. When can we take her home?"

"I don't know sweetie you will have to ask the doctor, but can I hold her for a minute" I said the little girl. She just smiled and nodded her head. I walked close and took the baby. The scent of him surrounded me but I ignored it. I never looked at him, but I can feel his eyes on me. The room got quiet as I held the baby. She was all smiles and goo goo's and at that I had to smile. Once I was done, I placed her back in Nemis's arm. I then kissed both their foreheads and walked out the room. I heard a whisper behind me but kept walking.

"Genesis" he called out to me. I turned and looked at him with the coldest look I can muster up. He just grinned and walked in my personal space. I took some steps back.

"What" I finally said.

"Why you are ignoring my calls and messages?"

"Because I have nothing to say"

"So, that's it you just going shut down on me like that?"

"What is it that you want me to do Rocky? I can't make you want me and I damn sure can't make you love me back so, the best thing for me to do is keep my distance besides I'm tired of your fucking rejection" I said then turned and walked away leaving him standing there alone.

Rocky

I have never felt so fucking low. When she walked out on me yesterday without saying a word it had hurt. When she ignored me it actually hurt. Through all that I thought she will get over it and today we can talk about it. Maybe I was being an asshole. I did have feelings for her I just needed her to know that I just can't pursue them because she shouldn't have to compete with a dead woman. Now, I feel like total shit. The pain I saw in her eyes made my heart clench and I was the cause of it. Believe it or not I never been the type to go around breaking hearts, but I broke hers. *Damn*. I then turned and made my way back into the room. What I saw was heart-warming. Star was sleep in Nemis's arms and Nemis was singing twinkle, twinkle little star.

"Nem give me the baby honey. It's time for us to go" I said to the little girl and held out my hands for the baby. I grabbed her and kissed her chubby chocolate cheeks while placing her in the bed and the doctor walked in. It has been three months since I lost my wife, my parents and a life that made sense.

"What's up doc?"

"Nothing Mr. Williams thank you for asking. She is looking good and if things keep progressing, I believe we can release her the beginning or middle of next week" he said. I nodded my head. That is some wonderful news. Maybe me and my girls can make our way to Wisconsin finally. But the thought of not seeing Genesis again nagged at me.

"Thank you" I said and looked down at Nemis who was beaming. That day we walked out the hospital with smiles on our faces. It didn't last long because before I knew it, I heard skid marks and I saw ski masks and guns pointing outside of car windows. Shot's was being fired and I instantly covered Nemis's body with mine. I heard her sobs and even though I wanted to retaliate with gun fire of my own I didn't and watched the car turn the corner, but I got the plates. It seems like my father's ghost has followed us to Alabama. I looked at Nemis and realized that her life was in more danger now than ever.

"Rocky, Rocky are you and Nemis ok" a familiar voice rang out. I still covered Nemis and rage took over me. I felt fingers pulling on my shoulders then I felt a kiss on my lips. My vision became clear at that moment and I was met with Genesis's scared eyes.

"Your bleeding" she said to me. I moved and looked at Nemis. She instantly threw herself in my arms.

"Nem, baby is you hurt" I asked the little girl all chocked up. God my father will kill me if I let anything happen to her.

"No, I'm fine but your bleeding" she responded back. It then felt like my shoulder was on fire. I pulled back the shirt I had on and long behold I was bleeding.

"Damn" I murmured. Then I saw someone running towards us and as I was reaching for my gun, but Ricky's face came into view. He held his hands up in a surrender type motion. That paused me. He dropped to his knees and looked at me through caring eyes. He then turned his gaze towards my sister and did a quick assessment of her.

"Come on, we need to get that bullet out" a soft voice said. I looked at Genesis and realized she was in danger to. I need to get them all away. I will hide them, collect myself then finish what my father and I started. All those muthafucka will die by my hands. The worst thing they could have ever done was come after my kids. The gloves were about to come off and I was about to strike a mighty blow.

I didn't fight Genesis as she led Nemis and I through the doors and towards the emergency room. Some old nurse wanted to take Nemis to a different room to have her checked out but the look I gave her let her know that I will snap her fucking neck if she even tried it. The doctor rushed in and tried to check me out first, but I pointed to my baby girl and he turned eyes to her. She had some scratches on her palms from when I landed on her but other than that she was fine. They cleaned them to make sure they didn't get infected. Then he came to me and had to pull the bullet out of my shoulder.

Once done he insisted that they admit me for observation, but I told him to just give me some damn pain medication, antibiotics and let me go on my way. Once I had my shit together, I grabbed Nemis hand and we made our way to check on Star. Ricky was standing by her door waiting on me. He knew what I was about to do. My baby was breathing on her own, eating and being a normal baby. I had to get her out of here. I had to get my girls to safety.

"Genesis, I need you to get her doctor in here. He needs to discharge her now" I said as I turned to her. My eyes took on its deadly state. My beast was close to the surface and if this doctor didn't do what I wanted I will lose all control.

"I can try Rocky"

"Now!" I shouted and she jumped back from me. I know I scared her, but I was too pissed to give a fuck. She didn't argue anymore however she turned and made her way to the nurse's station.

"Did you get the plate number" I asked Ricky.

"Yes, the car was registered to a guy named Micken Renalds. He is a native from Detroit. He ran with a guy named Deny. They have a major organization in Chicago called Money for Brothers. It's a major drug game organization but from the information my guy was able to pull up they have their hands in everything. Every member has a criminal background. Deny however is dead which you probably know. Anyway, the organization is now being ran by his three brothers Troy, Robert, and Gillian. There is a major price on your head as well as your sister's. As for Life for Whites they have concluded that you are responsibility for the life of those members. They knew that your wife was pregnant, but they didn't know if the baby lived or not. I was able to put a block on all the patient's records here, so no outsiders were able to get in and hack their data base. They have members of their organization that does that shit. This shit is getting too dangerous." he replied.

I nodded my head and picked up my phone to book tickets to Exuma, Bahamas. My mother always wanted to go there when I was younger but there was always something to do that stopped them from going. Now I needed to take advantage. I needed to get them somewhere safe. I on the other hand had no intention of leaving. Shit just got really fucking real for me. After booking the tickets I booked a penthouse villa at the Grand Isle Resort. I just hope Genesis can get off because now that her association with me might be known, her life hangs in the balance also. I'm not opposed to forcing her to quit her job though. Believe me when I tell you that both groups will gladly get rid of her just to piss me off. I can't allow that to happen. She is now my responsibility to. I started pacing because the damn doctor was taken so long. Just when I was about to shoot my shit Genesis and Star's doctor was walking towards me. I looked around for Nemis, but she was in the room standing next to Star.

"How can I help you Mr. Williams" he asked.

"I need you to discharge Star right now"

"May I ask why"

"No" I said in a deadly tone. He took a step back, but Genesis took a step towards me. I looked at her and calmed down some.

"Is she at risk for any health problems that can occur" I asked him. The look I was giving him was deadly.

"No, Mr. Williams I was just going keep her for more observation, but she is doing very well. She is at a healthy weight to where she can go home. She breaths on her own, eats on her own. She has no need for special attention" he responded.

"So, she can go then"

"If you need to yes. But I must warn you that there are some police officers in the emergency room trying to get a sense on what happened outside earlier"

"Police is no concern of mine. Is she up to date on her shots so far"?

"Yes, she has gotten everything she needs so far I have made sure of it. I am a pediatrician" he said.

"Okay, then please get the discharge papers" I replied to him.

"Okay I will make sure that you have all the information you need. Am I going to see her in my office?"

"No, so please make sure that I have all papers for another doctor. We will be leaving town tonight" I said to him. His eyes got wide but just nodded his head and walked away to find Star's nurse. I turned to Ricky and he moved to the waiting room on the floor. Then I looked at Genesis, she cocked her head to the side giving me an evil ass look. I know she still mad at me for rejecting her, but I will make it up to her when I get all three of them to safety.

"I need you to tell them that you have a family emergency and you have to leave for a couple of weeks" I told her.

"Rocky, I just can't up and leave my job and everything I worked so hard for" she replied.

"Genesis, you and those girl's lives are in danger. I need you to do what I say and how I say it, so I can get yall to safety. Besides you said you wanted a vacation so I'm going to give yall one." She just looked at me for a minute. Then she turned to walk away but stopped.

"I will tell them what you told me to say and I will follow your lead Rocky, but we have to talk. I need closure if things are not going to go any further with us. Speaking of vacation are you not going considering you said give us one" she said. When I didn't answer she walked away and left me standing there. If she thinks she's getting closure she got another thing coming. She just doesn't know her ass is mine now.

I checked the room to make sure that Nemis and Star was straight. Nemis was sleeping in the rocking chair next to Star's bed. Luckily, when I cleared out my condo, I put the baby's much needed things in the back of my truck and left them there. With that thought I walked out the room and to the waiting room to search for Ricky. I spotted him staring at the wall at nothing. I knew from the look on his face that he was in this full force with me. I knew that the moment I saw him at the funeral. I sat down and stared to. I was deep in thought and trying to come up with a plan. Both groups had the advantage. I didn't like that I couldn't do what I really wanted to do but the love I have for those girls were keeping me grounded. Maybe if I would have been a little more diplomatic my wife will still be alive.

Even though I really had no intention on going with them to the island, I realized that I needed time with my girls. I needed them to know that I put them above all else. Rage invaded my veins, but they invaded my heart. In that moment my decision not to go changed. I needed to be with them if only for a little while.

"Rick, I need you to take us to the airport in my truck. Then I need a trusted team of yours to clean out my suite and Genesis's apartment. Keep all her clothes and woman products but get rid of everything else. Take care of her lease and then drive my truck to Milwaukee. I will be taking the girls on a much needed get away. I will contact you two days before we are due to fly to Wisconsin with the flight information, so you can pick us up at the airport and, so you can make it there in time. I don't trust anyone else to do this. Besides things might change and I need someone to be open to those changes" I said to him. For some reason I felt defeated and that feeling had my beast on alert.

"I got you man. You know that" he replied to me. The look on his face told me that he was just as pissed off as I was, and he had a beast in him to, but the difference was my beast was a lot deadlier.

I then nodded my head, got up and walked back towards the room just when the discharge nurse for Star was coming down the hall and Genesis was behind her looking pissed still. I ignored her look and met the nurse in the room. She then did her last assessment of the sleeping baby and started to clean out the bottom of her crib putting the items in a green bag she walked in the room with. I then went to the bag that Nemis and I brought to the hospital and pulled out a full body long sleeve onesie. Genesis was now helping the nurse. Genesis then changed Star's diaper and reached for the outfit I had in my hands. Everyone was quiet as the nurses completed their tasks of preparing my daughter. Then the nurse turned to me and started talking a mile a minute. I was paying attention, but I wasn't. I was transfixed on Genesis and her interaction with the girls. Even though I may have missed some of the things the nurse said I am pretty sure that Genesis knew everything she said. She handed me the paperwork. Said bye to my three ladies and walked out the room. Before I knew it, Genesis was holding the bundled-up baby in one arm and holding the sleepy Nemis hand with the other. I grabbed both bags and picked up Nemis. She said nothing but followed me out the room and out the hospital with Ricky trailing behind us.

Genesis

When the plane was landing, I was struck with pure beauty. I have never seen a place more beautiful than Exuma. I was sitting by the window holding Star, Nemis was in the middle and Rocky was in the aisle seat. I was still mad at him. Luckily the hospital was understanding about the sudden leave of absence I had to take but I have a feeling that I will not be going back.

Okay, let me back up. When we made it to his truck, he turned to me and demanded the keys to my car and apartment. Of course, I wanted answers but the look in his eyes deterred me only for a moment. When the time is right, and he had a chance to calm down I will be asking what all this shit is about. Anyway, I gave him everything he needed. Luckily, I was able to keep my purse and shit. When we boarded the plane, he said nothing, I said nothing, and the babies was still sleeping. Once we got up in the air that's when Star was about to get buck wild but it's a good thing, I had what I needed, and I instantly took care of her. Nemis, was mad because she didn't have her back pack. Rocky kept telling her he will buy her more, but she wasn't having it. She kept frowning at him, and I don't think he liked that much. She eventually went back to sleep. About an hour into the flight they started serving food. I would have to say that I love first class. Plus, a damn drink was in order. When everything relaxed again. The bubbly baby and mad little girl closed their eyes again. I looked out the window but kept taking glances at Rocky. He was deep in thought but the look on his face was one of contentment.

When the plane landed, we walked through the airport and made our way to the rental car area. No one had anything but the baby. I wasn't worried though because I had money and I'm pretty sure he did to. We got in the car and made our way out of the airport Rocky pulled up a map of the island to locate shopping areas. We made it to a tourist strip mall in no time. Traffic was very light and accommodating. He treated us to a shopping spree. I tried to resist but he kept telling me to get whatever I wanted. Nemis on the hand got whatever she wanted. He brought things for all four of us and when I saw the total I almost died. Once we left that store, he found another store that sold baby items and stocked up on things that Star needed too. By the time we made it to the resort all of us was exhausted, but I wasn't too far gone to not notice the beauty of the Grand Isle Resort which contained a three-bedroom Lucayan Villa just for us.

During check in he informed the front desk that we needed a baby crib brought to the villa. When we entered the villa, I was at a loss for words. I don't know how much money this man spent on this, but damn do I appreciate it. Don't get me wrong I am not money hungry, but I can enjoy the beauty of this resort and his gesture in making this happen for us. On the flip side I do believe that he had to force himself into joining us. His mind is on revenge but the need to be with his daughters won that argument. Nemis announced her joy by screaming out loud, which brought me out of my thoughts and startled the baby. Star whimpered and Rocky scolded Nemis for her outburst. She didn't pay him any mind though. She went on about her business with a big smile on her face. I can't even begin to tell you how pleased I was with him or even describe the room, so I am going to skip that part.

Star was still in her car seat looking around when there was a knock on the door. The people who handles the bags was bringing our things in the room along with pushing the baby crib that looked brand new. Rocky said nothing but pointed to the room that he will occupy. Once they were done and they left, and he looked at me. Fire was in his eyes but so was tiredness.

"Thank you for this Rock" I whispered to him.

"Your welcome. Besides I believe we all needed this get away" he replied. Then he picked up the phone and ordered us some room service. He then moved towards the room Nemis was in. I picked up Star out her car seat and decided that we will be taken a nice bath this second before the food arrived.

When we were done Nemis was sitting in the living room area watching a kid movie already clean and in her pj's. Rocky was sitting next to her. I guess they resolved their differences. When I walked into view he got up and made the baby a bottle. I then feed the her and as she was getting finished the food arrived.

Things progressed like we were a normal family for the rest of the night. We ate, laughed and even cuddled. I enjoyed all it and prayed that he will let me have all of this. I found at that moment that there was no other place that I would rather be than here with my family.

When Nemis finally passed out laying on Rocky, he got up and tucked her in bed. I was feeding Star again, but he helped me move to his room instead of mine. He said nothing and I asked nothing. He then went to the bathroom to wash the day's grim off himself. When he emerged, Star was feed and dry. She was in the crib sleeping. He walked to her crib and looked at her. His eyes sparkled and I can tell that he was thinking about his wife. I felt kind of jealous but decided that I was being petty as hell.

When he looked at me, he looked conflicted but relieved. Even though those two contradicting looks confused me I was focused on his body. He was full of muscles and ripples. He had a towel wrapped around his hip. His breathing was even. It was like he has come to some sort of peace. When he finally walked towards me it was like he was stalking me. He was the predator and I was his prey. He surprised me though and sat next to me. I had on some pajama pants and a camisole type shirt that went with it.

"What's wrong" I asked him.

"I feel like I am betraying her Gene. But I can't help what I feel for you and I'm conflicted"

"Then, follow your heart Rocky but I won't be used, I'm done with your rejection. If we are going to keep this strictly about the kids, then let's do that. I'm not trying to make anything complicated for you and I'm not going to keep allowing you to hurt me either." I replied in a stiff tone. That statement made me mad. *How the fuck is he betraying her. I must compete with the damn dead.* I wanted to scream that statement at him but when I looked at him, he smiled. Then his face became serious again. He let out a heavy ass sigh and I can still tell that he was conflicted. Without a word he got up went to his bags and pulled out some pajama pants. He didn't even care that I was sitting there he just threw the towel on the floor and got ready for bed. He looked at me, but he looked pissed off. *Damn this man is confusing and sometimes I don't know what is right or wrong around him.* I shook my head went to the baby's bed kissed her then walked out and went to my own room. I smiled once I entered and closed the door because I did not miss that raging hard on, he had.

Sleep didn't come easy but eventually it did. I had no dreams, but I remember faintly around 3am a baby crying. I was so distorted that as I walked through the villa it sounded extremely loud. When I made it too Rocky's room Nemis was in the bed with Rocky trying to wake him and Star was in her crib screaming her little head off. Rocky was sweating and kept saying "don't leave me, come back to me." Nemis looked at me with panic-stricken eyes and I picked up Star. I sat on the side of the bed and rubbed my hand over his face.

"Bliss" he whispered. I pulled my hands back and stood up.

"Nemis come on honey, he will be ok" I said to her. She looked confused but kissed his check and moved off the bed as I grabbed the baby's diaper bag. I gave him one last painful look and walked out the room. There was no need for me to keep trying. His wounds are still fresh, and I understand that. But there is nothing in the rule book that said that I had to feel what I feel and continue to allow it to happen. So therefore, I made a vowel that I will no longer pursue him. I will just consider myself the nanny of the girls and that is the role I will play because at the end of the day those babies needed me to, and I will not walk away from them even though I throw in the towel with him.

Rocky

I woke to a very quiet room. That I didn't understand because I could have sworn that I heard my baby crying but I couldn't open my eyes. Shaking my head, I got up and sat on the side of the bed and looked at clock. It was nine in the morning. I got up and made my way to the bathroom and did my morning routine. I then walked out of the room and was greeted with an empty villa. Trying to figure out where they could have gone, I turned to get my cell phone but before I can call her, I heard giggles coming from the doorway as it opened.

"Where did yall go" I growled. Genesis said nothing but shook her head. Nemis looked at me like I crazy and Star cooed. I stood there waiting on an answer. My beast was standing there too. He wanted to fucking know. We needed to keep them safe and she is running off with my damn kids.

"Genesis" I said and slightly raised me voice.

"We went to breakfast down stairs. They have a buffet style set up down there" she replied but the look she gave me was impatient. I said nothing after that. Maybe I am overreacting. I sighed then turned to Nemis and smiled.

She mirrored my smile and ran to me wrapping her little arms around my leg. I then bent down and picked her up.

"Did you enjoy breakfast?

"Yes, it was good. I had pancakes." I chuckled, kissed her cheek then put her down. I held out my arms for Genesis to walk into them, but she just put Star in them and walked to her bedroom closing the door behind her. I looked at Nemis and she looked at me just as confused but shrugged her shoulders.

"Can we go to the beach today please" she asked in a sweet tone.

"Yeah sure why not. But first let me run down stair and eat" I said to her.

"Ok" she said running to the couch.

"Can you watch the baby for me" I asked her while depositing Star in her car seat and putting her binky in her mouth. I made sure to check her diaper then looked at Nemis. She was looking at me.

"Can you Nem" I asked again. She said nothing but nodded her head and turned back to whatever she was watching on the tv. I then straightened and looked towards Genesis bedroom door. Even though I wanted to go to her, I didn't. I walked out the door in search of a meal.

Once that was done, my lady's and I made our way down to the beach. It was already packed but we found a nice little spot under a tree. Genesis and Nemis instantly made their way to the water. I guess she was determined to teach Nem how to swim. Star and I just played by ourselves. While holding she bounced, cooed and giggled. Making me smile but I couldn't keep myself from thinking about the time my Bliss and I enjoyed ourselves in the water. I was so deep in thought that I didn't hear or see Genesis and Nemis come back to where Star and I was. I didn't even feel Genesis stares on me. My heart was breaking with every thought of the people my kids and I lost. The worst part was as much as I wanted to just wallow I couldn't. I had to turn all my pain into anger. I had to be strong for them but as much as I wanted someone to be strong for me, I just couldn't let her. She shouldn't have to compete with a deceased woman, but I wasn't ready to let go of my wife. If only she understood, if only she will be patient.

I finally snapped out of my day dream and turned my gaze to Genesis who seemed to never have taken her eyes off me. I just smiled at her, but that jester was not returned. She frowned instead, rolled her eyes and turned her attention back to the girls. I couldn't do anything but shake my head because as much as I wanted to be pissed at her I realized that I couldn't. She had every right to feel how she was feeling. So, I politely excused myself and made my way to a bar for a much-needed drink. *By the time I get done it should be time for lunch and naps.* That way I can make my way to the hotels bar and do some more drinking right along with drowning my own sorrows.

When I returned the girls were gone. I took a deep breath and stared out at the waters. I loved the peacefulness of it and made a promise to myself that I will walk the beach later tonight alone. I then turned and made my way back to the room where they were eating. Genesis was feeding Star and Nemis just looked like she was wearing out. I smiled at the view. They were all so beautiful.

"Come eat daddy" Nemis said in a tired tone. Without making her wait, I made my way to the table and enjoyed a quit lunch with my three ladies. Once the girls were down for a nap, I just left the room. I know I'm being a dick but at the end of the day I really don't want to face her wrath. Even though I deserve it. I picked up my cell and decided to call my father's mystery man. If Ricky couldn't find that compound, then he could.

"What's up Rocky? How have you been my friend and I am deeply sorry for you lose" he says.

"I'm good man and thank you. I know you did all you could to help. I really appreciate it. But look you know I'm not the one to beat around the bush. I need the location for the Life for Whites compound"

"You're out for blood aren't you"

"They killed my wife, of course I am"

"Is that all?"

"No, I also need the drop on the brothers of Deny and their main spot for their organization. Not only did they kill my parents, but my little sister has a target on her back. They had gunners ambush us at the hospital my daughter was at man. This shit needs to be delt with and fast. I refuse to lose my kids"

"Damn, man I had no idea. Ok, give me 48 hours and I will have all the information you need. Rocky, be careful my friend."

"Always and thank you" I said and hung up the phone and ordered me a Scotch on the rocks. Today I need the good shit.

It's kind of bothered me because I knew I was going to cut this vacation short, but I had no time to waste. The sooner I can end the threats the better off my girls will be. I'm not worried about myself. See, what many don't know is the first time Genesis showed me that she was willing to take up responsibility for the girls was the day that I had my dad's lawyer who has also been mine draw up papers of immediate guardianship. They will also be well taken care of as far as money. The house in Wisconsin is also in both our names. She has access to all bank accounts and the money my parents left me will immediately be turned over to her in any case of my demise. She would never have to work again. She will never have to leave them with anyone. To sum it all up what's mine is also hers.

As I sat there at the bar enjoying my drinks I thought about Genesis and Bliss. How they have the same morals and values, but so different. Bliss was so gentle and no where near hood. Genesis on the other hand has some hood ass characteristics about herself but carried herself like a pure lady. She was also gentle, but her attitude was ridiculous. Is it so wrong to feel what I feel for another woman so soon? Is it so wrong to want to move on, not only for my sake but for the sake of those girls? I know how Nemis feel about Genesis and to Star she will be her only mother figure. Why shouldn't I hold on to the happiness that was right in front of me? Who said that I had to mourn alone? As conflicted as I was, I made up my mind. I got up from the bar and made my way back to the suite. I was keeping my woman. Because losing her and my kids was not a fucking option.

When I made it back to the room, I found Genesis sitting on the couch by herself. The kids were already sleep and I guess she was waiting on me. At least I hope she was. I went to her and dropped down to my knees and whispered, "I'm sorry."

Genesis

He took me by surprise when he leaned in and kissed me oh so sweetly. Chills came over by body and I shuddered. When my brain finally caught up to me, I realized that he apologized.

"I'm sorry for hurting you Gene. Please forgive me baby. I don't want to lose you" he said. I was shocked I said nothing. But the look in eyes made my heart skip a beat. They told me that that apology and everything he said was true.

He then took matters into his own hands and led me to his room and proceeded to discard my clothes, but I stopped him.

"Are you using me again" I asked as tears pricked my eyes. I closed them just so they wouldn't fall they did anyway. I knew his eyes shown the truth, but I still had to ask.

"Genesis, look at me" he said. When I did his eyes softened and an emotion, I thought I would never see was there. Love.

"No, I am not using you again baby. I want to make love to my woman. You mean so much to me and I'm sorry it took so long to realize it. I was so stuck on thinking I was betraying Bliss that I couldn't see what she put in front of me." he groaned out and wiped away the tears. With that comment he kissed me. He finished removing my clothes and his. As he laid me down, with his body coming down on top of mine he rubbed his monster against my core and pure pleasure ran through me. My pussy was wet, and I was ready. He on the other hand wanted to tease my body. He rubbed me, kissed me, and ate my pussy like I was his last meal. When he then put his dick in me, he pushed in so slow I thought I was going to scream in frustration. Damn!!! I needed him to pound me, claim me and take possession of everything that I had to give. He didn't disappoint. He pulled out slowly but shoved his hips forward fast and hard. Every sound we made was getting louder and louder.

Then we heard a whimper and realized that the baby was in there with us. He smiled but continued his assault on my pussy. He covered my mouth with his and together we muted each other moans. He then adjusted his hips and pushed against me. A shiver ran through me again because he was hitting that spot. I dug my nails into his back leaving behind evidence of our animalistic love making and bucked my hips against his. Letting him know that I wanted more. Shit, I needed more. He gave it to me.

My body took on a pleasure I have never known before. Spots appeared in front of my eyes and my orgasm rocked me. I felt like I was flying. He never removed his mouth from mine, but his body stiffened, and I knew he deposited his seed into my body. When we both calmed down, he got off me and pulled me close to him. He covered my body with his and sleep took both us under. I felt so complete.

Rocky

I was hearing a baby cry, but it seemed like I couldn't open my eyes. I fought against the sleep and when I succeed, I realized that my baby was crying. Genesis was moving to disentangle herself from me, but I stopped her. I got out of the bed instead. I kissed Genesis lips then found some pajamas. I put them on and a white beater and made my way to Star. When she seen my face, she stopped crying and smiled at me. My heart melted. I love her so much. She reminded me of her mother. I picked her up and left the room in search of diapers and milk. When I had her dry and a bottle in her mouth, we deposited ourselves on the couch. Nemis, then walked out of her room and joined us on the couch. She snuggled up close to us and that's where we sat. When Star was done, I burped her and laid her on my chest as I stretched out. Nemis laid by my side closer to the cushions. I wrapped my arms around both of my babies and went back to sleep. That is where Genesis found us the next morning.

"Rocky" I heard someone call to me. When I opened my eyes the girls and I were in the same position. She looked pissed.

"You could have dropped the baby" she said.

"But I didn't woman. I knew she was there"

"Well, just be careful"

"Yes, mommy" I mocked. She gave me a crazy look and moved to the kitchen while me and the girls stayed where we were. Nemis's eyes was open and Star was getting some tummy time on my chest.

"Did you know that this kitchen was stocked with food" Genesis called out.

"Does that mean you're going cook? Nemis and I is hungry" I called back and my little Nem giggled. I guess she wasn't mad at me anymore which was good because I didn't like when she was. She then crawled around me and the baby and made her way to her room. Star started getting antsy and when I sat up with her Genesis was handing me a warm bottle. I changed her first then feed my Star. When I deposited her in her car seat she was drifting. By that time the villa was smelling like food and I went to open the doors of the balcony. It was a beautiful warm day. Even though my thoughts were on eliminating the threats to them my body was relaxed. More relaxed than it had been before my wife died. A vacation was what I needed but revenge etched in my blood.

By the time breakfast was over we decided that a stroll on the beach was in order. We packed up a bag of supplies that will hold us over for a couple of hours and left the room. Once there Star and I chilled out, while Genesis and Nemis got in the water. I held my baby in my lap and her mother's face came into view.

"She would have loved looking at you my dear Star. You remind me so much of her" I said to the babbling baby. She and Nemis was happy and that made my world alright. I held my baby close and looked out as Genesis and Nemis enjoyed themselves. Their smiles were infectious, and I couldn't help but smile myself.

We had a little picnic on the beach, and I can tell this was Nemis's favorite spot. When all else fails her in life I want her to always go to a place where she can find some peace. After the picnic and a little more play time we went back inside to put the girls down for a nap. We then deposited ourselves on the couch and that's where we fell asleep.

I heard the phone ringing and as I was waking up, I heard a sexy voice.

"Your phone Rock."

I grabbed and answered in a groggy voice. "Hello"

"I got that information for you"

"Damn you work fast dude"

"That's what I get paid to do"

"Ok, so what do you have for me then"

"They have their compound set up on this little dirt road out in a small town called Prattville. It's about 24 minutes out. The population is mostly whites and the other colors that do reside there try to stay out of their way, but they are terrorized all the time. Considering the compound is in a very private area they tend to have their monthly festivities close by. I will text you the address. And as far as Deny's brothers they set up shop in a low crime area called Norwood Park. They operate under a community-based organization called Help for the Youth. They have different programs for the youth of all age brackets. That is why they never been caught. It's crazy how criminals can teach children how to be upstanding citizens. Anyway, I will text you that address to."

"Thanks man I really appreciate"

"Just be careful man. Before your father was killed, he told me that he didn't want this life for you anymore that is one of the reasons they sent you to college. He also said that in his demise he knows you won't stop until you have your revenge. I said that to say this be careful because those children need you." With that the phone line went dead and two messages came through on the phone.

2448 W. Willow Road, Prattville, AL

10200 60th Street Chicago, Ill Norwood Park Area

It's time to play. I thought with a smile on my face. I wasted no time getting up from the couch and made the necessary arrangements for my departure tonight. I even texted Ricky the information I just received and the time I would make it to the airport. Knowing that he will have to catch a flight out himself back to Alabama. With a deep breath I turned and looked at Genesis as she called my name.

Genesis

Shit it sucks when you only get one half of a conversation. It also sucks ass that from his body language I can tell that what was being said was making him hyped up. I didn't know what to think but the look in his eyes seemed to change. His cat eyes glazed over like an invisible high was taken over him. His pants started to tent up. That was a beautiful sight though. I just couldn't help but wonder what is being said to him that is making his body react that way.

Once the phone hung up and a smile appeared on his face it was like I knew. He was entering his dangerous mode but not full force. He was allowing his beast some freedom.

"Rocky" I called out because honestly, I was getting a little scared. I know the girls and I are safe with him, but I truly have never seen this side of him before.

"It's ok baby" he replied. The tone of his voice was low but soft. He then turned his full glazed over eyes to me. Without warning he picked me up and walked to the bedroom closest to us which was my old room. He closed the door quietly.

"Genesis, I need you right now. Suck me off baby then I can explain everything" he said in a husky tone but still soft and low. Instantly I went down to my knees as he worked to free his raging hard dick out of his shorts. Once free my hands went to it and moved up and down while looking at him, he sighed.

"Genesis don't tease me right now" he growled out. Not wanting to agitate him I place the tip of his dick in my mouth and sucked, licked and kissed. Still teasing I know. He said nothing though and let his head fall back. I alone decided to stop playing and suck that monster into my mouth. I worked him up and down taking his further down my throat each time. He started rocking his hips and his hands curled up in my hair. My mouth got super wet and slippery as I continued to suck, and he started to thrust. I gagged when he pulled me down to far but never broke the rhythm that we created. As I continued and saliva started to run down my chin, his grip on my head tightened and I felt his body stiffen. Then seconds later my wet mouth was filled with spurts of cum. I didn't want it to go to waste so I swallowed it all, never spilling a drop.

Once his dick deflated and he pulled me up he kissed me. Tasting himself on me but never complaining about it.

"Let me brush my teeth Rock" I said. As soon as the words came out my mouth and he opened the door we heard a wail from Star and Nemis was sitting on the couch. He went to Star who was in the same direction I was, but I continued to the bathroom.

When I got finished with my chore and made my way back to the TV room, Rocky was holding Star and she was giggling away. He was blowing raspberries on her tummy. Nemis was watching the Disney channel. When he sensed me, he turned a loving gaze towards me and smiled.

"We will talk when I'm done with the baby" he said. I just nodded my head and joined them on the couch. There was a feeling of dread flowing through me, but I tried not to show it. I didn't want the girls to react to my stress and uneasiness. As I started to get into the movie Nemis was watching he put Star in her car seat and stood up. I followed him without being told to.

We got to the room and I noticed a look of apprehension on his beautiful face.

"What's wrong" I asked

"I have to leave" he replied. I froze at his revelation and my heart was beating fast.

"Why?"

"You know why Genesis. I need to eliminate the threats against yall."

"What? Rocky why won't you just let the police handle this? Why do you have to go and play superman?"

"Genesis first off don't insult me okay. I don't deal with police besides they don't seem to deliver the right kind of justice" he said. Then he paused and looked at me. Tears was shining but I was working on keeping them from falling.

"If I don't return in two weeks, there is a number saved under attorney in your phone give him a call and he will tell you all you need to know. If I don't return in that time frame just live, be happy and take care of our children. You will never have to leave their sides if you don't want too. But know that all threats will be gone" He said.

Anger started to boil and before I can stop myself, I blurted out "isn't this how you got your wife killed, leaving her alone to feed your sick desire to kill." I regretted those words as soon as I said them. Pain, confusion then pure rage crossed his face within seconds. His beast was standing in front of me displaying his full height and he was royally pissed off. Rocky took a menacing step towards me but stopped in his tracks. Before I could even apologize, he walked out the room. I stood there with tears falling down my face and feeling like pure shit. My heart was hurt because he was leaving us but also because I said something so hurtful that I may not ever forgive myself for.

When I stepped out of the room all three was no where in sight. I looked at the clock and realized it was dinner time. Not bothering to call them and see where they were at, I let them have their time together. I sat my stupid ass on the couch just staring at the TV and letting my mind take me in all types of directions. *I'm an asshole…*

Rocky

I have never wanted to hit a woman as much as I did Genesis at that moment. She brought up the fact that my wife is dead because of me. That shit stung. I didn't need a reminder to know that her death is on my hands. The guilt eats me alive every time I look at my daughter. All the horrible shit I did in life has tainted my soul and that is on me. Losing my parents and my wife is on me. One thing is for damn sure I refuse to lose my children and my woman even though she just pissed me off. My beast must go to war again.

Dismissing that shit I walked over to my kids and gathered them up. I decided that taking them to dinner in the hotel restaurant would ease some of the fucking anger in me. Their presence always seems to calm my soul. I just needed to enjoy the little time I had left with them because in four hours I will be leaving them. Dread filled me as Nemis talked and laughed, Star cooed. Both warmed my heart.

Once we made it back to the room Genesis was not on the couch and that was ok. I needed to say goodbye to my kids. I looked at my baby as I sat on the couch with Nemis and she gave me the prettiest smile a father can ever ask for and my sister looked at me like she knew something was up but smiled anyway. I knew I had to tell her that I was leaving for a while and I wanted them to enjoy their paradise.

"Nemis, I have to leave yall here for a while, but I will be back" I said to the little girl whose eyes showed worry and fear. This shit hurt me for real because she has been through more shit than a normal adult.

"Daddy left and never came back Rocky" she replied, and tears developed. I pulled her onto my lap and held her and Star kissing both of their foreheads. I never been the type to make promises that I couldn't keep. The truth of the matter is I might not come back and honestly that is ok with me because I know that I am leaving them with someone who will take care of them. I also know that I am tired of this life. My parents wanted something better for me even though I bucked them. Now, all I can do is hope and ask the most highs to spare me this one last time and let me live that life they wanted. If not, then let me join the woman I lost to that life. Either way I am fine with the outcome.

"Nem, I love you and Star with my everything. Just remember that ok" I replied to her. She nodded her head and I kissed her cheek and planted her back on the couch and setting Star in her car seat. When I stood up Genesis was standing by the bedroom door. I said nothing. I just looked at my kids one last time and walked out the door to catch my flight.

As I got in the cab that was waiting for me, I decided that I needed to make sure that everything was on point on Ricky's end. I gave him all the information that was given to me about the location of both groups.

Rocky: Are we all set?

Ricky: Yes, I will see you at the airport

I sat back, closed my eyes and allow the little bit of peace I do have take over. My beast is close to the surface and he wants to fucking play. The crazy part is so do I. I'm finally about to get my fucking revenge. I'm going serve that shit cold, painful and with a promise of fucking death.

Rocky

As the plane was descending, I became more alert. Imagines of my parents and wife started flooding through my mind and pure red clouded my vision. I wanted to catch those muthafuckas off balance. Ambushing them is the only way to go because that's what they did to me when they took my wife.

As I existed the plane the imagines disappeared, and my beast was in control. I Rocky no longer controlled my actions. Beast is the one who is running shit now. I made my way through and out the airport in record time finding Ricky standing by his black SUV. We exchanged greetings then got in the car. That's when I noticed three guys in the back dressed in all black. I grinned because it's funny how muthafuckas in the military can get wild too.

In twenty minutes, time we made it to what niggas in the "D" will call a chop shop. Inside was loaded with all types of weapons that literally made my dick hard. On top of that it was ten extra niggas. Don't get it twisted we may be short in numbers, but we are the most dangerous.

"Black" I said to Ricky

"Your outfit is in the office towards the back" he replied. I went straight there and changed into my signature colors. Taking a deep breath and allowing my body to take it's state I walked back where the group was. As I made it too the room all talking stop, and everyone looked at me. I'm a predator at heart and even though these niggas were dangerous I alone was the deadliest and I smelled fear.

"Relax" I said with a sadistic grin.

"Look guys, this is Rocky he is the one leading this mission. We go in and kill everyone besides woman and children" Ricky told his crew.

"They start training their boys at age 10 to hate" I said. I started pacing back and forth because a child was a child, but hate is something I can't tolerate right now. That hate took my wife from me.

"My crew is not killing any kids Rocky" he said sternly. I looked at him like he lost his mind but, in the end, I agree with him. As much as I want to end this group and anyone who is in it I can't and won't take the life of a child.

"Look we get in and out. I don't have time to linger or wait for anyone to second guess themselves. This shit has been a pain in my ass long enough. Once we hit the road, we cut all lights. I don't want those muthafuckas to know that death is at their door knocking. When all the threats have been eliminated everyone will check in. There is fifteen of us in total. If one does not check in your ass will be left. This isn't no man left behind type shit. From my guy there is a main cabin on the left that houses the main leader of this group. That is the only one that will be riding out with us. That kill is MINE. Let's load up" I said, and orders immediately got followed.

The ride to the compound was fast. Everyone was suited in all black with bullet proof vest and black ski masks. Once the lights where cut and all vehicles came to a stop shit happened fast. Everyone existed their vehicles, gun trained and moved in like this shit was a raid. Instantly gun shots rang out and I left that shit to them and made my way to the cabin. Stupid muthafucka left his door unlocked. I walked in and felt the hairs stand up on the back of my neck. When I turned around there was a woman standing there with a shot gun trained on me. Her pale face was full of fear.

"Woman don't make me hurt you, drop the gun"

"Leave" she replied with a shaky voice.

"Have it your way then" I replied and moved so fast she didn't even know what hit her. I snatched the gun out the bitch's hand and wrapped my hand around her throat. I have every intention on chocking the life out of her.

"Mommy" I heard and instantly I dropped that bitch like a sake of potatoes. I squatted down to look her in her fucking eyes.

"Today is your lucky day. Where is he?" I said to her. She tried to buke me but the look I gave her made her rethink her decision.

"He ran out the back door when the guns started going off. There is a shack about 50 yards in the woods" she replied looking at her child. Shaking my head, I got up and ran out the back door in search of the coward who will leave his woman and child behind.

Finding the shack was easy, without thinking I just walked in and took a shot to the chest. Even though I stumbled back I didn't fall. He tried to shoot his shot gun again, but I was too fast. I disarmed him like my ole' dude taught me to do a long time ago and repeatedly punched his bitch ass in the face. Once he slumped, I let his ass fall. Immediately I tied his ass together with zip ties and dragged his ugly ass back to our starting point by his hair. I looked towards the cabin as I passed it and the woman was standing there holding a tiny little girl that I heard but didn't see.

"Thank you" she yelled out to me leaving me shocked but not confused. He left her to die by my hands and she would have had it not been for that little girl. Now they are free to live their lives without this coward.

I threw his ass in the back seat and sat near him. My body was humming, and my unusual state was present. Shit, it showed its face when I saw all those guns.

"Check in" I said in the comms I had on. Instantly all the men started calling off.

"Anyone injured" I asked.

"Nah, we are all good and headed back to the vehicles" Ricky announced. I grinned but turned to look at the shithead that was still knocked out beside me. *If only he knew what I had in store for him.*

When everyone was back in the SUV's we got the hell out of dodge because the sounds of police sirens were ringing out loud. It's a good thing we knew a back way out the fucking area. It's also a good thing that I decided to put on a fucking bullet proof vest.

Ricky

The car was full of silence and I had to keep looking at Rocky in the rearview mirror because his breathing was extremely accelerated. The amount of rage coming off him was unbearable. There was another one of my guys in the back seat with him and the hostage and even he kept eye balling him.

"Hurry the fuck up" he growled out and I knew he was close to snapping. Don't get me wrong I understood. We broke all speeding limits to get to the shop so he can play because I really didn't want any more blood in this truck.

When we pulled up, he jumped out the car before it even came to a complete stop. He paced back and forth taking deep breaths. I tried not to look at the complete profile of this nigga because for whatever reason his body was doing some strange things. Considering this is not the first time I seen him in this state I wasn't too surprised, but my men was confused as fuck.

"What's up with your man" one of the men asked.

"He lost a lot because of this group man so let him do what he does. Besides a raging beast can be dangerous to everyone if he doesn't get a handle on it" I replied and with that he grabbed the leader of what used to be The Life for Whites Organization out of the truck and disappeared to the play room that he specifically said the shop needed to have.

Everyone shook their heads unloading weapons and changing clothes when we all heard a fucking scream.

Rocky

I took the pussy to the play room and laid his ass on the bench that was there. I cut off the zip ties and tied his ass to that muthafucka with the harshest rope Ricky was able to find. There was a small blow torch in the corner, and I grinned. I took my knife out of the back holster on my pants and began to cut open his clothes. His fucking son rapped and beat my wife. The rage I felt was so strong I was able to taste it. Once I had his ass bare, I woke his ass up by pissing on him. Yeah, I know it's gross but shit I have no water, so I had to improvise.

"You are fucking nigger" he spat out once he woke.

"How dare you piss on me, you are fucking animal" he contorted again.

"Shut up bitch. You can't take a little urine, but my fucking wife took a beating and rape from your bitch ass son and his cronies. Then you have the fucking audacity to keep coming after me and mine. You're going die today" I said and gave him a deadly look. He pissed himself. This nigga was just full of piss.

Not wanting to prolong the inevitable I took the blow torch and started roasting his penis like it was a fucking marshmallow. That muthafucka screamed like a girl. The smell of burning flesh assaulted my senses and I smiled.

"Whoa!!!!" I screamed out getting more and more excited.

"Now, how are you feeling man" I asked.

"Just kill me already"

"Nah, I am enjoying myself" I replied to him. I then set the blow torch on his ass again. Screams ran all through the shop and my dick is hard as a fucking hammer right now. I turned it off after a while. His ass was still breathing. Smiling I walked around him. He was looking at me through glassed eyes and charred skin. Yeah, his ass was stepping on deaths door.

"Nice knowing you my nigga" I said as one last taunt. One thing about chop shops is you can always find a weapon. I lifted a pipe up high and brought it down with all my might on his fucking head. The sound of bone splinting, and crushing ran out. Blood splattering the walls and on me. His brains were seeping out which only fueled my sick desire. The pipe itself was sitting in his head sticking out on both sides. The satisfaction I received from this kill was sicken.

I existed the room and was met with a bunch of eyes. Some full of fear, others full of disgust, *probably from the burning flesh smell* and some full of confusion. I knew what I needed to do because my body was calling. Without saying a word, I made my way to the bathroom. Pulling down my pants in a hurry I gripped my dick and Genesis's mouth came into view. As I stroked I new it wasn't going to take long. My balls drew up and I sprayed me cum all in the toilet.

"DAMN!"

Genesis

I tried my best to keep a calm demeanor around the girls. I didn't want them picking up on my vibe, especially Nemis. She is so smart and good at reading people. She must take after her dad and brother in that department.

Getting through the day after Rocky left was challenging. The children seemed to be extra agitated. Nemis was throwing temper tantrums, which she normally never does. Star was crying more than she usually do. I was very overwhelmed but for them I did my best and kept calm.

When things finally calmed down and I got them in bed I cried myself. Not only was I hurt but I was tired. I never knew what being a parent was really all about until I had to be one by myself. Maybe that is why I am so emotional. I am alone trying to mother two children while my man is out there killing people.

I know I probably sound like I don't understand but in all reality I do. I shouldn't have said what is said because that was just wrong. I understand that he must secure these girls safety. I understand that he has scores to settle and his rage and pain will consume him if he doesn't. I guess I just didn't want him to leave us. But now I sit here with worry.

I don't know if he is alive and safe. I don't know anything.
I tried calling him, but it keeps going straight to voicemail.
I tried texting but they are going unanswered. The only
thing I can do is be the mother I know I can be and hope for
the best. Hopefully he knows that my heart is calling for his
safe return to his family.

Rocky

When I finally pulled myself together, I went back out to the area where the rest of the guys were. Two of the men was dragging the dead racists out towards the back woods. Nothing hides a body like woods and wild animals.

"Guys I wanted to thank all of you for risking your lives tonight. Tonight, we settled a score for my wife. She was an innocent that lost her life due to these people and I really appreciate your help" I said.

"No problem man, anytime" they all replied to me in unison. I then motioned for Ricky to follow me outside and he did.

"Look I'm going to go to the motel and get some sleep. The drive to Detroit is going to be a long one."

"I'll see you in the morning man" he replied.

"You don't have to dude. This is a totally different fight" I answered back to him.

"Roc, this isn't about you. This is about an innocent here. I refuse to let you fight this fight alone when it means just as much to me as it does to you. I lost my sister too. So, I understand this is for your sister and your parents" he said with a hint of sadness in his voice. Nodding my understanding I turned and left for the night. I refused to take any cars with me, and a good walk is what I really needed. Besides the motel wasn't too far from my current location.

As I was walking, I pulled my phone out of my pocket and turned it on. There was a text message and voicemail from Genesis.

Genesis: Are you Ok?

I ignored that and called my voicemail. I missed them already. I was mad at her but not anymore. When I killed that dude, I realized that I did understand her concern. But I left them unreachable for a reason.

Genesis: Hey it's probably night where you are but I wanted you to know that I am sorry about the shit I said. I didn't mean it baby. I love you and our girls so much and I really don't want anything to happen to you. I know that this is something that you must do in order to move on and I get that. The only thing I ask is that you return to us safe and sound. This place is truly a paradise, but we can't enjoy it without you. I love you baby. Call me as soon as you get a chance just to let me know you're ok. Please Roc.

As much as that message touched my heart, I couldn't respond back to her. I needed to stay focused on the task at hand. A distraction can be fatal to all of us and I refuse to let anyone else in my family become a fucking casualty.

Troy

That nigga Rocky is becoming a pain in my ass. He dropped off the grid for a minute, but I was able to get this nerdy ass dude that did some work for me back in the day. He was able to hack this nigga's phone when he made it back to the states. I knew he was gone, and he took that bitch and those brats with him.

I had some nigga in Alabama looking for that fool and they let me know when he showed back up. I was then able to have my nerd put a virus on his phone that literally gave me access to all his information. I was kind of disappointed when he couldn't get me the bank information. That nigga doesn't mobile bank. Any who, I also was able to get him to clone the hospital number that his female work at so I can get that bitch to come back.

I could have had my men that was in Alabama to go at him, but they are a bunch of pussies. He will off them all. Besides, this shit is personal and the situation with him needs to be handled by my brothers and me. Without thinking I had this little red bone bitch I used to fuck with call her.

"Hello"

"Yes, may I speak to Genesis please?"

"This is she"

"Hi, my name is Christi and I am a nurse here at the hospital where you work at and your boyfriend Rocky Williams was brought in today with a gunshot wound to the back. You are listed as his next of kin and I was wondering can you come down to the hospital and sign some papers."

"Oh my god! Is he going be ok?"

"Well, it's looking pretty grim right now. How soon can you get here?"

"Well I'm not in the states right now but I will be on the first flight out tonight. I will come straight to the hospital as soon as I touch down and please if anything changes before, I arrive please, please call me".

"Will do and I will see you soon."

When she hung up the phone, I had to put a sloppy ass kiss on her lips for her performance. Now let the games begin. Justice will finally be completely served, and the revenge will be ever better.

Genesis

I waisted no time packing up the clothes for the girls and I along with booking our tickets back to the states. I knew he shouldn't have gone back. I knew him coming back to us was a very low chance. Don't get me wrong I know my man can hold his own, but I would rather him to walk away from the revenge than to let it kill him. He didn't listen to me though and now he is hurt.

Before I knew it, I was at the airport getting ready to board the plane. Nemis was looking grim and worry line nard at her pretty little face. That made me feel guilty. These kids have lost so much it will be a shame to lose him to when they just got him.

Once we were seated, I closed my eyes and asked the most highs to look after him. Then I sat back and let the plane take us to where we needed to go. I looked at the girls, Nemis got comfortable in her seat and Star in my lap before I knew the sand man took them under and I let my mind take me to places with a better ending. A new beginning is what we needed, and I'll be damned if I allow anyone to take it from us.

Rocky

When I made it to my motel, I made my way to the shower. I had to get the smell of burnt skin off me. Now that my adrenaline decreased that smell was starting to make me sick to my stomach. That shit was fun though. I never turn an enemy into a piece of burnt meat before. Shaking my head to get that image out, my thoughts turned to my family. I would have to say that I came a long way. But that is neither here nor there I just want to get back to them. Trying to clear my mind I laid down and let todays excitement take me under.

I woke a couple of hours later with a sense of dread. Something just didn't feel right to me. I tried to ignore it and shake it off, but the feeling continued to grow, and I started to get uncomfortable. Not wanting to believe that my family was in danger I pulled out my phone and called Genesis's phone. It went straight to voicemail. I then started thinking about the time zone and told myself that they were safe. I made sure of that. I left them where I knew no one will get to them. I then closed my eyes again but that feeling nagged me more.

Giving up on sleep I kept trying to call Genesis. I prayed to the most highs that they were safe, but I kept calling anyway. It was around eight-thirty in the morning when I finally gave up and knew that something was wrong. I showered again and was making my way out of the motel by nine-thirty when I received the call.

"Hello?"

"Why so grim this morning Rocky man?"

"Where are they dude?"

"I have them. We need a trade"

"What's that?"

"You for two"

"It's three of them man"

"Well, you know I can't let one of them go. She must die to. I am a gentleman though, I can wait to kill her until you arrive"

"You're a funny ass dude. But I am sure that you really don't know who you are fucking with. If you touch a fucking hair on her head, I am going to cut your dick off and feed it to you"

"Are you really threating me, and I have the lives of your family in my hands right now?

"Humm… You must be Troy? Yeah my ole' dude put me up on you. Look if this is a power trip you are on right now then that's fine brah but understand if you wanted to kill them you would have. You want me. I alone pose the biggest threat to you and your family's empire. So, let's make matters fair. You let them go now and you won't know what dick taste like"

"Damn dude you almost had me going but your right about one thing I can kill them, but I do really want you. So, again let's trade"

"I'll be there in a couple of hours I am driving. Put Genesis on the phone"

Damn I hope he don't rape her.

"Rocky! I'm sorry…"

"Shhhh Gene it's okay baby. The little shit is craftier than I though. But look keep those girls close and I'm coming to get yall ma. Just hold on ok"

"Ok… Rocky I love you"

"Kiss my babies for me"

Then I hung up the phone. Yeah that was probably a fucked up move but I'll tell her when I'm in front of her.

I looked at Ricky and he knew what was up. Without a word he started driving.

"Look I have a jet I can use to get us there quicker" Ricky said.

"Nah, man. He doesn't want them. He wants me" I replied.

"How can you be so sure?"

"The conversation. If he really wanted them dead, they will be. I was with my father that night when his brother was killed" I said in a low tone. My vision was getting blurry and I was starting to feel light headed. I really didn't understand how I allowed my family to get caught up in this shit. I don't regret the path I chose because revenge had to be served but now, I'm just starting to feel like my lose will be greater.

"This drive will give me time to think of a way to get them out safely" I said to him. He didn't reply. Even though I knew what I was going to do. I just needed to be sure. I have every intention on a trade considering he really wants me. Well, let the games begin. *Bliss baby I'm coming to join you!*

Troy

Boom!!! Chaos erupted around me without me even being able to prepare for it. Thinking back maybe kidnapping his family was a bad idea. I remember my brother telling me how dangerous this dude was before him and his father took him out, but I guess I didn't believe him. Now here I am twelve hours later after our conversation I am fighting for my life. All I wanted was to avenge my brother.

Honestly, I had no intentions on killing the kids and his girl. He thought the target was him and his sister, but it was all about him. Yes, the little girls' grandparents had to die because they knew their dad. Other than that, I'm a family man myself. I used that as a ruse to get him here faster than his original plan. Now from the looks of it I may not make it back to my wife and daughter. It's okay though because what I live by, I am also ready to die by. I'm sick of this life and the drama it brings.

I wanted out of the game's years ago, but my brothers are relentless. They wanted me to step up and lead in the case of Deny's demise. Which don't get me wrong I love my brother, and may he rest however he is, but that nigga was evil. He was the one who wanted the child dead because of the betrayal of a bitch. He was the one who kept fucking with that ole Detroit nigga because of some bitch. The more I told him to let that shit ride the more he went after dude. Now, he is dead and my loyalty to my family may just cost me to my life. I know I was saying some other shit a little way back but it's funny how a nigga's tune switch when he is faced with death. It's sad because I am just now thinking of my own family, but this shit must continue and whatever happens, happens. Peace is all I am looking for anyway.

Rocky

Just when you think a muthafucka is ready for you a flaw on their part is revealed. Let me take you back. On the car ride I called all my hitters that used to work for my dad and gave then the location to the restaurant ole dude and I ate at before we took down Deny. I had put a plan in motion. Really, this shit was about getting my family out safely. I made sure that Ricky knew that his task was always to get them to safety and stay with them. He nodded his understanding. I then, let my hitters know the toys they needed to bring with them. That gave my dad's right-hand dude a laugh because that nigga likes to play.

Wait, I know you are probably wondering who all these niggas are but that is irrelevant. Anyway, everyone is to hit hard and fast. No stone is to be left unturned. At this moment every man in my squad was ready to die for the innocents

Now, back to the hear and now. When that first bomb went off, I knew then that this shit was about to get real. Ricky went one way to find my family I went the opposite to end this evil as line of brothers that has caused so much drama for my ole dude. Gun fire was going off around me, people was dropping like flies. I even heard one of the brothers call out to Gillian as that nigga took his last breath. Yeah, my dick was on ten. That bullet belonged to me.

I found the other three brothers hiding behind what look like large canisters. Shit we can all die in this bitch it really made no difference to me.

"Damn! My nigga I wasn't expecting you this soon" Troy said in a mockery type tone.

"You have something I want. Where are they?" I asked this fool in a deadly tone.

"Dead bitch" he replied. I laughed because this nigga knew damn well, they weren't. He clearly underestimated me though. Do you remember the policy I had about woman and children? Well, right now that shit was thrown out the fucking window.

"Okay" I replied and made a phone call.

"Kill them" I said to the person on the phone.

"What? Kill who?" Troy asked. His breathing has increased, and panic struct him. I was able to smell that shit. Shit when a nigga think they got the upper hand I sometimes must remind them that I am always in control of shit.

"Your wife and baby girl. See, when you decided to fuck with mine that's when all bets were off my nigga. If you would have left my family out of this shit then, yours will be untouched" I taunted him.

"Your fucking lying" he screamed. His brothers then got reckless and started shooting. I hid behind the wall I was up against and let them rain bullets. When they stopped, I returned the fire hitting one in the head and the other in the chest. They dropped like the rotten ass potatoes they were.

"My wife and kid man?" I heard Troy ask me.

"You started this shit" I replied. He turned towards me and started shooting nonstop until he emptied his clip. When I went to return that fire I paused. Genesis was walking up behind him with the look of rage in her eyes and a gun she must have taken off someone. She had a nice black eye and tears was streaming down her face. I lowered my gun as she aimed hers to the back of Troy's head. We locked eyes and she pulled the trigger. Brains splatter all over her face. As his body was dropping, she drops the gun and started running towards me. Before I knew it, I heard a female scream and when I turned, I saw a gun being pointed at Genesis as she got closer to me. Without thinking I ran towards her and pointed my gun at the woman and fired. Two shots rang out, Genesis and I hit the floor.

I felt a burning sensation in my side and my vision blurred. Not from damn tears but from the pain. I blinked then opened my eyes again to this beautiful brown face with silky hair telling me to stay with her. She was crying. I felt hands on my wound, but I also felt myself going numb.

"Help me" I heard her scream. I then hear running foot steps and familiar voices that I grew up hearing telling me to hold on. That they were going to get me to the hospital. The visions of my kids face came to mind and I smiled.

The next thing I knew I was in a car with my head in Genesis lap. I smiled at her. She was so beautiful.

"Don't you dare leave me and these kids Rocky" she said in a teary voice.

"Take care of them Gene, and I love you to baby" I replied to her. Then Everything went black. *Peace at last....*

I had to be dreaming because my Bliss was standing in front of me. She was still disheveled but still gorgeous. How I was so ready to join her?

"No! It's not your time Rocky. Baby you still have a lot of life to live. Your story must continue" she said.

"Bliss no dammit, I don't want to go back. I'm tired of it all ma. I need peace."

"And you shall have it my love but just not here with me, not yet. Don't worry, I will be waiting for you" she said. And with that she disappeared.

Epilogue (Rocky)

It's funny how things work out. I thought that the peace of death was finally going take over, but I was wrong. Apparently, life has some more work for me to do. I know you are probably interested in when happened after I woke up and if I really had Troy's family killed or not. Ha, I told you before I don't kill innocent woman and children.

See, I did go to her house and had every intention on a trade. His family for mine but then the fear in that woman's eyes and the look of his little girl made me change my mind. I know I can be heartless but I'm not a monster. We talked and she told me that she wanted away from him and that life. She wanted to raise her daughter. This woman was far from stupid. She just didn't know how to get away.

See she has been stashing money away for a while and she had enough to live off until she got settled. So, Ricky and I set up a plan to help her. Peace is all that some people want, and I get that. She got out. But I did need her to stay with one of my men until I tricked that nigga into acting out in pure desperation. Once that kill them call came through, she knew that she had a clean break without that fool finding her or her child. They were already on the highway being drove to where ever she wanted go.

As for me when I opened my eyes there were some ugly ass man over me saying welcome back. I had to close them back because that nigga was making my eyes hurt. When I woke up again, I heard the voice of a little girl and ohhs and ahhhs from a baby. A smile instantly formed on my face as I turned my head to look at my kids and my woman.

"Don't do that to me again" Genesis said. Then she kissed my lips. My kids looked at me with pure love and hopefully forgiveness. This takes me to where we are today. I hope your ass is ok with the short version I gave you because I have shit to do.

As I look out the window at my family, I realize how lucky I truly am. Even though I was ready to die, at this moment the will to live is so much stronger now. The house I brought in Wisconsin finally has its occupants in it. My wife Genesis who is currently pregnant with my little man and my two daughters. That's right, even though Nemis is my sister and because my father left her to me Genesis and I was legally able to adopt her. Ricky went back into service he felt like his job on that aspect wasn't over. That man will always be my nigga. So, Bliss was right my story continues but with the peace that I have always wanted. It was her and my parents sacrifice that made this happen and because of them I will always have love in my heart and loyalty in my soul. But, please don't get it twisted I am always ready to handle some shit when need to. Besides I have been noticing something dark and dangerous inside Nemis. The girl tends to travel else where in her mind and the dark glaze over her eyes take root. Whatever it is hopefully I can catch it before it gets out of control. Besides that, I just want her to enjoy being a child. Do me a favor though, stay true to those who are true to you and to yourself.

Made in the USA
Las Vegas, NV
22 July 2022